D0183743

SPECIAL MESSAGE TO READERS

THE ULVERSCROFT FOUNDATION
(registered UK charity number 264873)
was established in 1972 to provide funds for research, diagnosis and treatment of eye diseases. Examples of major projects funded by the Ulverscroft Foundation are:-

- The Children's Eye Unit at Moorfields Eye Hospital, London
- The Ulverscroft Children's Eye Unit at Great Ormond Street Hospital for Sick Children
- Funding research into eye diseases and treatment at the Department of Ophthalmology, University of Leicester
- The Ulverscroft Vision Research Group, Institute of Child Health
- Twin operating theatres at the Western Ophthalmic Hospital, London
- The Chair of Ophthalmology at the Royal Australian College of Ophthalmologists

You can help further the work of the Foundation by making a donation or leaving a legacy. Every contribution is gratefully received. If you would like to help support the Foundation or require further information, please contact:

THE ULVERSCROFT FOUNDATION
The Green, Bradgate Road, Anstey
Leicester LE7 7FU, England
Tel: (0116) 236 4325

website: www.foundation.ulverscroft.com

THE CAPTIVE CLAIRVOYANT AND OTHER STORIES

The Baker Street Irregulars, the gang of ragamuffins who sometimes assist Sherlock Holmes in his investigations, put their wits and courage to the test against kidnapping, robbery and murder . . . A boy announces that he has seen a ghost, but the truth is far more terrifying . . . A gypsy seeks vengeance from beyond the grave . . . An ancient evil awakens and desires fresh victims . . . These five stories of mystery, horror and the occult from the pen of Brian Ball will thrill and chill in equal measure.

Books by Brian Ball
in the Linford Mystery Library:

DEATH OF A LOW HANDICAP MAN
MONTENEGRIN GOLD
THE VENOMOUS SERPENT
MALICE OF THE SOUL
DEATH ON THE DRIVING RANGE
DEVIL'S PEAK
MARK OF THE BEAST
THE EVIL AT MONTEINE

BRIAN BALL

THE CAPTIVE CLAIRVOYANT and Other Stories

Complete and Unabridged

LINFORD
Leicester

First published in Great Britain

First Linford Edition
published 2014

A catalogue record for this book is available from the British Library.

ISBN 978–1–4448–1832–1

Published by
F. A. Thorpe (Publishing)
Anstey, Leicestershire

Set by Words & Graphics Ltd.
Anstey, Leicestershire
Printed and bound in Great Britain by
T. J. International Ltd., Padstow, Cornwall

This book is printed on acid-free paper

Contents

The Captive Clairvoyant

1

If Mr. Sherlock Holmes had been in the country when the Baker Street Irregulars stumbled across the mystery, which I have called The Case of the Captive Clairvoyant, then no doubt he would have given immediate assistance.

But Mr. Holmes was in Switzerland engaged in a deadly duel of wits with his most feared opponent, the evil Professor Moriarty; and so the Baker Street Irregulars, the gang of ragamuffins who sometimes assisted Mr. Holmes in his investigations, had to rely on their own wits. I, Sergeant Hopkins, had taken it upon myself to record the investigations in which the great Sherlock Holmes was employed to only a limited extent — those not described by Dr. Watson.

It all began — and — ended — in the theatre where Sparrow was employed, Trump's music hall.

That week there was a mixed bag of

acts. There was Signor Maccarelli, who threw knives; Gorgeous Gertie, who sang sentimental ballads; Madame Pompadour the comedienne; and a magician; but the star of the show was The Amazing Marvin, as he was described:

'Marvel at the Mystic Powers of Marvin', so the poster invited passers-by, 'Hypnotist Extraordinary! Mentalist Supreme!'

'Ah, excellent!' beamed Mr. Trump to Bert the doorman as he saw the packed house. 'Marvin's still bringing them in. Another week of this and who knows — I could get him to play to royalty!' And he clicked his heels as he rocked backwards and forwards with satisfaction.

'Marvin's good,' agreed Bert. 'Sparrow!' he yelled. 'Placards for Mr. Marvin — he's on in fifteen minutes!'

'Right, Bert!' called Sparrow.

'Get me a drink!' yelled a large lady from one of the dressing rooms. 'Be quick, Sparrow, darling!'

Sparrow sometimes thought he needed three sets of legs and hands. He was a general dogsbody for the artistes as well as a sweeper-up and an assistant scene-changer, but his principal job was to make sure that the placards which announced each act were properly displayed on the stage before the artistes began their acts.

'Gin and polly coming up!' he cried to Madame Pompadour, who was in need of a drink before her act. 'I got the placards ready, Bert!' he yelled back to the doorman.

'How's the new boy shaping up, Bert?' Mr. Trump asked.

'Sparrow?' said Bert. 'He's a good lad, very obliging and quick, and he's popular with the artistes, especially young Mary.'

'Is that so?' Mr. Trump said, frowning.

'I'll tell him to keep away from her if you like, sir,' said Bert, anxious to oblige his employer.

'No, don't do that,' said Mr. Trump. 'He isn't doing any harm. Anyway,' he said, catching sight of the small figures, 'she might need cheering up.'

Bert saw the small pale face of the girl, whose bright red dress emphasised her pallor. Then Bert looked at her huge, staring eyes.

'No,' agreed Bert, swallowing nervously. 'She do stare so, don't she, Mr. Trump?'

Mr. Trump shrugged.

'Marvin needs her in the act — but she's a trouper and she's got to bear up. The theatre's a hard place, Bert, but it's our living and Marvin's and the girl's too. But you can let the boy talk to her. And Bert,' he added.

'Yessir?'

'Let me know if he hears anything interesting from her, will you?'

'Such as what, Mr. Trump?'

'Oh, little things, you know. Nothing special — I just feel rather concerned for her. But you'll remember what I said?'

'You can rely on me, Mr. Trump,' said Bert as Mr. Trump went to the front of the house. 'Now, what does Sparrow talk to her about?'

Sparrow was listening, not talking; and as he listened he realised that Mary was the unhappiest girl he had ever known. He hadn't sought her out that evening — by chance he heard her sobbing in a darkened doorway where she had gone to hide her tears. And, so it seemed, from Marvin.

'He's getting ready for the act,' she told

him. 'He'll call me soon — and I sometimes think I shall go out of my mind when he sends for me!' Sparrow had spoken to Mary on a dozen occasions, but no hint of her mental torment had come out before tonight. He was totally perplexed now, for there seemed to be no reason for her misery.

'It isn't all that bad,' said Sparrow. 'Cheer up, Mary!' But her sobs shook her body.

'No one knows what it's like, being with Marvin!' she sobbed. 'He puts on a kind face when there's anyone around, but I think he really hates me!'

'But he can't!' said Sparrow in astonishment. 'He's your dad!'

'He's not, he's my stepfather, and my name's Mary Ashley, and I've been with him for only a few months — he met and married my mother in New York and learned the act from her, then she died almost as soon as he learned the routines. And he keeps me because he needs me, but he's cruel, terribly cruel!'

'I can't say as how I likes him much,' said Sparrow. 'He's got a nasty look about him.'

'He's evil! I know it!' cried Mary Marvin.

''Strewth!' said Sparrow. 'It is bad, ain't it?'

'I wish with all my heart I could get away from him!' the girl cried, and Sparrow was shocked by the force of her feelings.

'Well, I should leave him!' he declared.

'Leave him?' said the girl slowly, and her great eyes stared back at Sparrow, so that he felt uncomfortable and somehow afraid. She put her hands to a silver locket on a chain round her throat. 'How can I leave Marvin?'

Sparrow had never known his parents, so he told himself he wasn't in a position to offer advice; not at the time, anyway.

'No, I see it would be difficult,' he said. 'Him being your dad, your lawful dad anyway. And you being a successful star and all that. And anyway, you're American, ain't you?'

But Mary was staring past Sparrow now. He looked behind him quickly and saw the tall figure of the hypnotist.

'None of those reasons keep me with

Marvin,' replied the girl in a dead sort of whisper. 'You don't understand the power of a man like him — how could you? But he is evil!'

And, as she spoke, Marvin beckoned.

Like a well-trained animal, Mary silently went towards the tall, sinister figure, then they disappeared into their dressing-room.

'Now what was all that about?' whispered Sparrow.

He remained where he was in the shadows for a few moments, then he walked softly along the corridor.

Their dressing room door was open slightly, showing a chink of light and allowing Sparrow a view of Marvin and the girl. It was Marvin's voice, though, that caught his attention.

'You will keep it safe,' Sparrow heard, and Marvin's strange, deep, vibrant voice made him shiver. 'Always safe — and secret!'

Sparrow's natural inquisitiveness was reinforced by his concern for the girl, so it was inevitable that he remained to watch and listen. Marvin's voice was strange enough, but his actions were stranger.

He was facing Mary, who was seated with her back to Sparrow, but Sparrow could see her face in the big dressing-room mirror. In his hand, Marvin held Mary's silver locket by the chain.

It swung before her in a glittering arc, backwards and forwards. 'Remember!' came that weird, deep voice. 'Remember, Mary — you will stay with me and keep our secret. Do you understand, Mary?' Sparrow could not have entered the dressing room — not, as he told Wiggins and the others later, for a handful of gold.

And when he heard Mary speak in a strange, unnatural voice, he wished himself outside in the chilly, rain-soaked streets — anywhere rather than in the music-hall. For Mary looked as if she were possessed by demons.

'I obey you,' she said. 'The secret is safe!'

Then, in a moment, Marvin smiled a tight-lipped smile and snapped his fingers. 'Wake, Mary!'

The girl jolted forward and put her

hands to her head.

'It's almost time for the act,' Marvin said. 'You've been asleep, Mary — now, snap out of it, you little idiot, and put some make-up on. We don't want people thinking you're some kind of dummy, do we! Hurry it up, kid! Here, put your Ma's locket back on!'

'Yes,' she murmured. 'Mother's locket,' she said, tears in her eyes.

'Ah, The Magical Marvin!' cried Mr. Trump as the hypnotist appeared with Mary. Sparrow jumped back from the doorway instantly.

'Just giving Mr. Marvin a call, sir!' he cried, and Mr. Trump nodded to him.

'Good, good — don't forget what I told you, Marvin,' he went on to the hypnotist. 'You could be playing before the Prince of Wales himself soon!'

'I'm not too sure about that,' muttered Marvin.

'But you have a wonderful career ahead of you!' Mr. Trump enthused. 'And you too, my dear,' he told Mary.

'Chin up, I'll think of something,' hissed Sparrow as Mary went past him.

But Mary stared in front of her like a sleepwalker, and it was obvious that she had not heard him.

From the auditorium, Sparrow heard the loud applause as Marvin began his mystifying act.

'Ladies and gentlemen!' called Marvin, in his deep, vibrant voice. 'I have made the study of Mentalism my life's work, and tonight I shall show you the amazing powers of Hypnotism!'

There was a roll of drums and the crash of a cymbal, and Sparrow snorted loudly, for Marvin was passing his hands before the painted face and staring eyes of Mary, his stepdaughter.

'I shall show you,' declared Marvin, 'when I have put Mary here into a deep trance and blindfolded her, how I can communicate with her by the transfer of thoughts — by mind-reading!'

Sparrow watched as Mary apparently became drowsy.

'Now for the blindfold!' Marvin cried. 'And, if you are ready, ladies and gentlemen, I will ask you to find some object you carry about your person for

Mary to identify!'

Mary appeared to be in a deep trance, though she was smiling straight back at Marvin.

'Mary, are you asleep?' called Marvin, and in a slow, deep tone quite unlike Mary's normal voice she answered:

'I am asleep, Master!'

'Oh no you're not!' muttered Sparrow from the wings where he was watching the act. 'You were in a trance in the dressing room, but you ain't in one now!'

But the audience was impressed. There was a deep, sighing sound, and in the silence Marvin's voice rang out:

'Who will be the first, if you please? Who will ask Mary to identify an object — which she cannot see!'

Someone stirred. Then another, and another. Marvin pointed at a man who held up a watch:

'You, sir! I can see what you are holding, but Mary cannot. Mary!'

'Yes, Master?'

'Tell me what the gentleman is holding in his hand! Concentrate, Mary . . . Take your time. Are you ready?'

'I am ready, Master!' Mary said, putting her hands to her temples.

'Then what is it?'

'It's a — a watch!'

The audience gasped, then they clapped and finally they cheered. Mary identified a wallet correctly, and a ladies' purse; a handkerchief, and a gold ring. She was right every time.

'I reckon,' whispered Sparrow to himself as the curtains closed, 'that I know how you work it, Marvin — and it ain't Hypnotism or Mentalism, it's just plain faking!'

Gorgeous Gussie brushed past Sparrow.

'Get my placards up, duckie!' she called. 'Why are you staring at her?'

Sparrow jumped to fetch the placards. 'She's in trouble, that girl is,' he told the singer. 'I just wish I could do something to help her.'

'How sweet of you, duckie!' cried Gorgeous Gussie. 'Whoops — there's my cue, I'm on!'

She tripped on to the stage and left Sparrow still looking down the corridor, which led to the artistes' dressing rooms.

'I will do something to help Mary!' he promised himself. 'But I'm all at sixes and sevens over this business. Maybe Wiggins will know what to do!'

2

But later that night over hot peas and faggots in the cellar of the derelict house which was the home of the Baker Street Boys, Wiggins for once had little to say.

Normally he would have been excited by the thought of a fresh puzzle. When he got the smell of a mystery, he would look up at the picture of Mr. Sherlock Holmes and say something like, 'Now, what would he do?' or better still, 'We have our methods, Mr. Holmes and me, so we do!'

All he said, however, when Sparrow had finished telling him of Mary's hatred and fear of her stepfather was:

'It ain't much to go on, is it, Sparrow?'

'What!' cried Sparrow, swallowing rapidly and burning his throat in the process. 'She's in mortal terror of her life!'

'Blimey!' shivered Rosie, who was the youngest of them all. 'Who'd want a stepfather what does that to you?'

'Not me!' said Queenie. 'And if Mr.

Holmes was here, he'd soon do something about it!'

'Yeh!' Beaver cried. 'Mr. Holmes always helps those what's in danger, especially young ones and females. Sparrow ain't stupid, and if he says the girl's in mortal fear, then she is! And we've got to do something — so there!'

The rest of the Baker Street Boys joined in loudly, but Wiggins stayed silent for what seemed like hours.

'What do you think, Wiggins?' said Rosie, for Wiggins was staring at the features of the Master and she sensed that he was coming to a conclusion. It took some time in coming, though.

'I dunno,' said Wiggins at last. 'But I can tell you one thing for certain.'

'What's that?' said Sparrow.

'We've got to get Mary away from Marvin.'

'Wow!' they yelled, delighted that Wiggins had finally decided to act, especially Queenie and Rosie; for there was something particularly horrifying about Mary's plight which they felt they understood better than the boys.

'But that's not all we're going to do,' Wiggins went on. 'Mr. Holmes and I have our methods. We like to find out what's at the bottom of the mystery, and that's what we're going to do. If Marvin's got some nasty secret, like Sparrow says he has, then we're going to find out what it is.'

'Pheww!' said Sparrow. 'So what we going to do, Wiggins?'

It didn't take Wiggins long to explain. There was a lot more to the Amazing Marvin than met the eye.

When Sparrow said he wasn't going to try to meet Marvin in the eye because he'd seen what Marvin could do, Wiggins agreed that they should be extra cautious.

'Yeh,' agreed Queenie. 'This hypnotism business is dangerous, Sparrow. You watch out for yourself in case he gets his nasty eyes on you!'

'You're going to have to be very careful too, Queenie,' said Wiggins.

'Me?' said Queenie.

'Yes,' said Wiggins.

'Why, what's Queenie got to be careful for — she ain't going to get Mary away from Trump's Music hall, is she?' said Rosie.

Queenie gazed at Wiggins for a while.

'You're planning something nasty, ain't you, Arnold Wiggins?' she said, but Wiggins wouldn't tell her any more.

All he said was:

'We have our methods, me and Mr. Holmes.'

3

Sparrow was kept even busier the next evening. Everyone seemed to want him to run some errand or other. Bert made sure that he helped the stagehands, and Mr. Trump too seemed to be checking up on him continually.

'So you like working here, boy?' Mr. Trump said, as Sparrow waved to Gorgeous Gertie who was about to begin her first song. 'I see you're a friendly sort of fellow — the artistes seem to like you.'

Sparrow tried not to let his glance stray to a large basket, which usually held the magician's stage-effects.

'Yessir,' said Sparrow, who for once was almost at a loss for words.

'And Mr. Marvin's daughter, er, Sparrow,' said Mr. Trump, 'I believe you talk to her sometimes.'

'Yessir!'

Sparrow trembled. What was Mr. Trump getting at? Had he heard Mary telling him that she was desperate to get away from the hypnotist's evil power? But Mr. Trump merely nodded approvingly.

'I like to see a boy that tries to get on with people,' he said 'How does Mary like it here in England — does she speak much of New York?'

'Nossir!' said Sparrow. 'I didn't know she come from New York.'

Mr. Trump frowned and clicked his heels. 'Get on with your work,' he ordered, and he walked away.

Mary was already searching for him backstage.

'Sparrow!' she called, in a low, tearful voice. 'I can't stand it any longer! But every time I try to run away my head starts to swim around and I can't drag myself away from the dressing room! And yet I must go. I know that Marvin's about to do something dreadful! He keeps yelling out for no reason at all, and he stares out of the window all the time, wherever we are . . . '

'Careful!' Sparrow gulped as he heard footsteps, but he glimpsed Madame Pompadour's green chiffon dress and went on:

'I gotta be quick — I know how he keeps you with him, and it's to do with your head swimming all the time.'

Mary's white face looked haunted.

Unconsciously, her hands wandered to the locket at her throat.

'I dream of it too,' she whispered. 'I hear his voice, and I see something shining in those terrible dreams.'

'He does it with your locket!' snarled Sparrow. 'I saw him last night — and he's not doing it anymore!'

'Who's not doing what?' called a deep voice.

'Blimey!' gasped Sparrow. 'It's Marvin!'

'What are you doing here?' growled the hypnotist suspiciously. 'Are you spying on me, kid?'

Sparrow protested his innocence, but it was Mary who saved him by telling Marvin that she had asked Sparrow to fetch her a drink.

'OK, OK,' Marvin growled. 'Just keep away from the kid, OK?'

The evening seemed to drag by on leaden feet as Sparrow waited for the right moment; and eventually it came. He waited then for the explosion that must follow.

Sparrow was in the wings on the far side of the stage from the artistes' dressing-rooms when he heard the commotion. Voices called urgently — Mr. Trump, Marvin, Bert, and a couple of stagehands, all of them calling increasingly loudly so that they could be heard above the sound of the orchestra.

Mary had disappeared!

'Gone?' said Sparrow innocently, as Mr. Trump crossed the stage towards him. 'Who's gone?'

'Sparrow! Where is that confounded girl?' cried Mr. Trump, heedless of the calls from the audience, who were expecting the curtain to rise on the hypnotist's act. 'Where is she?'

Marvin spotted Sparrow too.

'Say, kid,' he called, joining the manager. 'You were talking to Mary — where's my daughter?'

'Search me!' said Sparrow. 'I ain't seen her for a half-hour or more — not since you said I was to keep away from her.'

'Damnation and blazes!' yelled Mr.

Trump. 'I've got a theatre full and no act! I've got to have Marvin's act!'

'And I've got a daughter that's cut loose!' yelled Marvin. The orchestra leader poked his head through the curtains.

'And there's a restless audience out here, sir,' he called to Mr. Trump. 'What shall I do?'

'Don't look at me,' said Marvin. 'No kid, no act — she knows the routines! I'll go and look around for her.'

Mr. Trump looked around wildly.

'Fetch Gorgeous Gertie back!' he called. 'She'll have to do another turn — tell her it'll be another five guineas!' Then he turned to Sparrow. 'Now, boy — '

But Sparrow was not there anymore.

* * *

'I can't believe it!' Mary cried when Sparrow led her into the cellar of the derelict house. 'I'm free!'

Queenie and Rosie rushed to bring her to the warmth of the fire, whilst Sparrow grinned triumphantly. As for Wiggins, he simply looked smug.

'And these are your friends — all orphans, like me?' said Mary, gazing around her curiously. 'I'm so grateful to you all!'

'It was Wiggins' idea to use the magician's chest to hide you,' said Sparrow. 'And it worked a treat, didn't it, Mary?'

'Oh, I heard Mr. Trump yelling at them to look everywhere, and when they banged on the basket — ' began Mary.

' — and looked inside — ' went on Sparrow.

' — and got fooled though I was in there all the time — ' gasped Mary, who managed to laugh now at the memory of her ordeal.

' — and then we waited till everyone rushed outside, and here we are,' finished Sparrow, looking fondly around the cellar. 'Home, sweet home.'

'And I'm never going back,' said Mary. 'Never!'

'Course you're not,' agreed Wiggins. 'Mind you, Marvin's not going to give up the act, is he? Not when there's royalty coming to see him. He's going to keep on looking for you, Mary, but when he doesn't find you, he's going to want a new girl for the act.'

Mary shuddered.

'I wouldn't wish that on any poor girl!' she said.

'Yeh!' shivered Rosie. 'What girl'd be fool enough to go on stage with Marvin?'

Wiggins looked from Mary to Rosie; and then to Queenie.

'But we've got to get to the bottom of this mystery,' he said. 'Ain't we — even if it does mean one of us working with Marvin?'

Queenie let out a long gasp.

'One of us?' she cried. 'Working with Marvin — Arnold Wiggins, if you're thinking what I think you're thinking — '

'Queenie, this is our most important case!' declared Wiggins. 'What's a bit of danger for the Baker Street Boys? You wouldn't mind being a star of the music-hall for a night or two would you?'

'Yes!' cried Queenie. 'I won't do it! You can't make me — anyway, I can't do this Mentalism business — and I won't be put in trances!'

'Don't let that worry you,' said Mary. 'Marvin doesn't put me in a trance on stage. It's all a fake.'

'I thought it was!' said Sparrow.

'So you could teach Queenie here the routine?' asked Wiggins.

'In five minutes,' said Mary. 'But don't let her do it! It's too dangerous!'

By now, though, Queenie was won over to the idea. She was an independent-minded girl with a strong character; and she had lived by her wits all her fifteen years.

'Wiggins is right,' she said briskly. 'I'll be able to find out what your stepfather's really up to once I'm his new assistant. Now, what about this here routine?'

It was easier than any of them — except Sparrow — could have imagined. There was no hypnotism, and no trance — nor could Mary peep through a concealed hole in the blindfold.

It was all done by means of code words. Mary explained it all.

Marvin would blindfold her after he pretended to hypnotise her. Then he would call on members of the audience to hold up some object. There wasn't much variation in the objects they produced. It would be a watch, say, or a wallet, or a handkerchief, or a ring — and Marvin had a code for each item.

If it was a watch, he'd say to Mary, 'Now, Mary, think hard — take your time . . . '

'So 'Time' was the code-word for a watch,' said Mary. 'It's as easy as that.'

'Elementary, my dear Mary, as Mr. Holmes would say,' agreed Wiggins. Mary smiled at him.

'Of course it is,' she agreed. 'For a ring, Marvin would say,

'Concentrate, Mary, don't let your thoughts wander around . . . ' '

''Around'!' said Sparrow, as Beaver frowned. 'Get it — 'around'. 'Round! A ring's round, ain't it?'

Queenie soon picked up the routine, and it was decided that Sparrow should introduce her to Marvin the next day at the music hall. It could hardly have gone better, though at first Marvin had his doubts.

'That brat of mine never makes a mistake,' he told Sparrow and Queenie when he had got used to the idea of using her as a substitute for Mary. 'You say this kid's worked in the music halls before?'

'You try her out, Mr. Marvin, sir,' said Sparrow. 'She knows all the tricks, don't you, Queenie — here, put the blindfold on.'

'OK, OK,' said Marvin. 'We've got the cops looking for Mary, but so far she's not shown up — I got to have an act for tonight, so let's try something. You ready?'

'I'm ready,' said Queenie.

'I'm holding up an object,' said the hypnotist, holding up a silver cigarette case. 'Come on now . . . concentrate hard . . . Queenie . . . '

'I know!' cried Queenie. 'It's a silver case — a silver cigarette case!' Marvin relaxed.

'I guess that's one problem solved,' he said, but he looked a desperately worried man. 'OK, Queenie, we'll go through the whole routine, and if you know it, we'll play the show tonight. This is one performance I can't miss — not when there could be royalty coming!'

Sparrow bumped into Mr. Trump as he

left Marvin's dressing room. 'Well, boy,' he said anxiously. 'How did it go?'

'Smashing, sir!' Sparrow told him. 'Queenie's on tonight.'

'And no news of poor Mary?'

'The bobbies haven't found a trace of her, Mr. Trump,' Sparrow said, and as Mr. Trump turned away he muttered, 'And they're not going to!'

Sparrow was kept busy until it was time for Marvin's performance; and when he next saw Queenie he could scarcely recognise her. She wore one of Mary's red dresses, and her face was covered in stage makeup.

'Blimey,' said Sparrow as she and Marvin passed him back-stage. 'What do you look like?'

'Like a professional performer, Sparrow,' said Queenie, as the music struck up. 'Now, shut up and let me concentrate — wish me luck!'

Queenie hardly faltered.

She identified watches, rings, wallets and handkerchiefs; and her lively manner went down well with the audience. Sparrow was delighted for her, but he was watchful. Wiggins had emphasised that they were involved in a mysterious case, and that he and Queenie should be ready for any developments. But nothing out of the ordinary had happened so far.

'Now, who will be the next to try the amazing powers of Mentalism?' boomed out Marvin's deep voice. 'You, sir? You wish to request this blindfolded girl to identify something — will you pass it up?'

Sparrow craned forward.

'Is it a watch again?' hissed Madame Pompadour, who was watching the act with him.

'No,' said Sparrow. 'I can't see — bit of paper, I think.'

'Ah!' said Marvin, taking the paper.

And then he seemed to stagger as he looked at the object.

'What's the matter with him?' said Madame Pompadour. 'He's gone as white as a sheet!'

The audience noticed Marvin's discomposure too: and the musicians craned forward to watch him.

Seconds passed.

'I am ready, Master,' said Queenie, who

also realised that the silence had gone on too long.

'Yes!' whispered Marvin, who recovered himself quickly. 'It was a note — nothing to do with the act,' he said, raising his voice. 'I'm sorry for this delay, ladies and gentlemen — another object, if you please?

'Yes — you, sir. Fine!'

'Now what was all that about?' said Madame Pompadour.

'Search me,' said Sparrow.

'Was it that note?' she said.

'I dunno,' he answered. 'But it didn't do him any good, did it?'

Queenie knew that there had been a disturbance of some kind during the act, but she had no way of knowing how affected Marvin had been. 'How did I do?' she whispered as the act came to an end amidst the applause and cheers of the audience. 'Did I do something wrong?'

'No, kid,' said Marvin, hustling her towards the dressing room. 'You did fine — now, keep out of my way!'

He was so nervous and agitated that she became alarmed and edged towards the door. All Mary's warnings came back to her; but Marvin paid her no attention. He rushed about, throwing clothes into a suitcase, and looking out of the window every few seconds. And then he noticed Queenie at the door.

'Don't open that door!' he yelled.

Queenie panicked and yanked at the handle, but Marvin had her by the neck and flung her across the room before she could escape. He bolted the door and turned to her.

'Don't move, kid — OK?' he snarled. 'I gotta get out of here, fast!' He dashed to the window and used his strength against the frame, but the window wouldn't budge.

And then a crash came at the door.

'Help!' screamed Queenie as she realised that Marvin was terrified of someone — someone who was breaking down the door!

Marvin turned as the door burst free and a huge brutish form rushed in. Even in her terror, Queenie heard the loud blast of music from the stage that heralded Madame Pompadour's act — no one would hear the commotion, she realised. But nevertheless she screamed again.

A blow sent her reeling, and she knew little of what followed. She was aware of a struggle; of a desperate scrabbling sound; and then she felt herself seized roughly and raised. After that, a damp cloth blocked her breathing, and the last thing she could identify was a sickly, sweet smell — and that was all, for a long time.

4

I, Sergeant Hopkins, was in an excellent position to follow the exploits of the Baker Street Boys during the progress of the Case of the Captive Clairvoyant; for I was called to Trump's Music hall to assist my boss, Inspector Lestrade, in a murder investigation.

Murder? Yes! Marvin lay on the floor of his dressing room with a knife in his back; and as for Queenie, she had completely disappeared!

'I never did hold with this hypnotism business,' Inspector Lestrade murmured to me as we inspected the corpse.

'It didn't do Mr. Marvin much good either, sir,' said one of the many onlookers who had crowded into the room.

'What!' said the Inspector. 'Who's that boy?'

I recognised him as Sparrow, one of the Baker Street Boys, but I merely said:

'One of the theatre's staff, sir — the buttons, I believe they're called.'

'Don't trouble me with that now, Hopkins,' the Inspector told me. 'Clear these people out and we can get on with our investigation. Get statements from them all, will you?'

'That's Signor Maccarelli's knife in him!' called out one of the artistes, a large, stout lady.

'Is someone accusing me?' cried an Italian.

'Mr. Marvin wasn't liked,' put in Mr. Trump. 'He was a nasty piece of work.'

'It's my knife, yes!' Signor Maccarelli called above the hubbub. 'But I kill nobody, ever!'

'Hopkins, get them out!' Inspector Lestrade called to me. 'And I want you all to know,' he said as the artistes were driven out, 'that I believe I shall be able to solve this mystery only when the police are able to find the whereabouts of Mary Ashley, Marvin's missing assistant!'

Wiggins was in the corridor with Sparrow when Inspector Lestrade made this statement.

'But Mary's not involved in this here murder!' gasped Sparrow.

'Shut up!' hissed Wiggins. 'Listen!'

'Yes!' Lestrade finished. 'I think that young lady's deeply involved! In fact, I intend to have a warrant issued for her arrest!'

'On what charge, sir?' I asked him.

'Murder — accomplice to murder, Hopkins! I suspect that young lady of being in league with whoever murdered her stepfather! From what I've heard, she had no reason to love him — and the man's dead!'

Sparrow couldn't restrain himself. He rushed forward to the Inspector and cried:

'And what about Queenie — she's gone! She's been taken away and maybe murdered too — the window's open! That's how she was got out!'

Inspector Lestrade took a closer look.

'Now I recognise you!' he cried. 'You're one of Sherlock Holmes's amateur detectives — and if I'm not much mistaken, Hopkins, there's another one down the corridor — why, it's Wiggins!'

'So it is, sir,' I said to my boss.

'I will not have amateur sleuths about me!' cried Inspector Lestrade. Then another thought struck him.

'Hopkins — that girl, Queenie. Don't tell me she's also one of that gang of ragamuffins?'

'I'm afraid so, sir. Do you think she has been seized? She could be in danger, Inspector.'

'Not her!' said Lestrade. 'No doubt she's run off in all this commotion. And that's just what these other ragamuffins can do. Get them out, or I'll have them put in the cells for obstructing the course of this investigation!'

Wiggins and Sparrow were soon evicted by a burly constable; and when they stood in the rain-swept street, Sparrow said dejectedly:

'It wasn't such a good idea, was it, Wiggins? The bobbies will be hunting for Mary, and Lestrade's warned us off — there ain't much we can do, is there?'

Wiggins drew Sparrow under the light of a gas-lamp. He pulled a piece of paper from his pocket and showed it to Sparrow.

'That's the paper Marvin had on stage!' said Sparrow. Where did you get it?'

'Picked it up in the dressing-room as we was ordered out,' said Wiggins. 'You told me what happened on stage when Marvin turned white, and I just saw it lying there when Lestrade gave us the push.'

'Not much on it, is there?' said Sparrow.

'Enough,' said Wiggins.

'Just one spot — what is it, rust?'

'Blood.'

'Blood!' gasped Sparrow. 'What's it for, then?'

'I've heard about it,' said Wiggins. 'It's the final warning from gangsters and such-like — it's the death-spot from a gang.'

Sparrow passed the slip of paper back. 'So Marvin saw it and tried to run!'

'Yeh,' said Wiggins. 'But he wasn't quick enough.'

'Nor was Queenie,' said Sparrow. 'We've got to find her!'

'If she's alive,' said Wiggins.

5

Queenie awoke to find herself tied hand and foot, and with a gag in her mouth. She tried to roll over and discovered that she was lying on some kind of couch; there was a little light from the door and when her eyes got accustomed to the gloom she discovered that she was in a small box room.

It was musty and cold, and she had never felt so alone or afraid. This was worse in a way than the sudden shock of Marvin's violence, and then the brutal blow from the burly thug who had hit her and then chloroformed her — for she recognised now how she had been silenced.

Thoughts tumbled endlessly through her mind. She struggled against the cords at her feet and wrists but they would not give a fraction of an inch; she was trying to chew through the gag when a rough voice came to her from the next room.

‘Hello, sir. You all right?’

‘Of course! What about the girl?’

Queenie concentrated: there was something about the voice that was familiar; but it was muffled by the door and it was very faint too; the other speaker stood much nearer to her.

‘The girl?’ the familiar voice said.

‘Sleeping still — tied hand and foot and gagged. Will you take a look, sir?’

‘And have her able to identify me? Certainly not! Now, get back and find what I told you to find!’

‘I can’t go back there!’ cried the rough voice ‘ — it’s full of bobbies!’

‘It will be locked by now, and the theatre’s deserted — do as I say!’ the second speaker snarled, and there was the sound of a heavy blow. ‘Marvin had it with him! Find it!’

‘All right! All right — I’m going! But what about the girl in there?’ cried the thuggish voice.

Queenie had been following the conversation in an almost trance-like state. She knew she was being held captive by desperate men; but why and where was beyond her — except that it must be to do with Marvin, for both speakers knew him. It was also clear to her that the man with the rough voice was the thug who had knocked her down, and that the second speaker was his employer.

But what did they want from Marvin's dressing room? In the midst of her fears, Queenie had one consolation: Wiggins was right again. What better way of discovering Marvin's secret could there be than to become his assistant?

Queenie froze again though when the next words came to her: 'How about her?' grunted the thug before he left.

There was a pause, and Queenie heard a strange metallic sound. She couldn't identify it, but she had heard it before. It went on for several seconds. Terrified, she held her breath; for she knew her fate was about to be decided.

'How about her?' the thug had said. He meant, 'Do we let her live?' — Queenie was sure of it.

'Let her sleep,' said the second man eventually. 'We can see to her later.'

Queenie's breath came out in a long,

deep sigh behind the gag. She heard the slam of a door and two sets of heavy footsteps.

'See to me?' she whispered to herself. 'I can see to myself! And she started to test the knots.

* * *

Wiggins had just finished telling the other Baker Street Boys about the blood-spot, when the door burst open and a tall, thin man stood framed in the doorway. He was poorly dressed, and yet for all his sudden and frightening entry, he didn't seem particularly threatening.

Wiggins grabbed a poker. Mary let out a scream; Rosie grabbed her. Beaver put his big fists up. And Sparrow stood behind Wiggins with a chunk of wood in his hands — whilst Shiner stood behind him.

'What'd you want?' yelled Wiggins.

'It's OK, folks!' the stranger called, a smile on his face. 'No cause for alarm!'

'He's an American!' said Sparrow. 'Like Mary!'

'And I've seen him before!' said Wiggins. 'Who are you? You was near Trump's Music hall earlier — have you done anything to Queenie? 'Cos if you have — '

'Here, hold it!' the stranger cried. 'I'm on your side, kids, especially now I've found Miss Mary Ashley here! Cards on the table, OK — I'm O'Neill, Special Investigator for Pinkerton's Detective Agency. See, here's my card!'

'You look, Wiggins,' said Sparrow, so Wiggins cautiously approached O'Neill.

'It looks genuine,' he said.

'It sure is — and I happen to know about you kids working for Mr. Sherlock Holmes, so maybe you can trust me to come in and talk?'

Wiggins still hesitated. He turned to Mary.

'Mary,' he said. 'What do you think? Do we listen to him?'

O'Neill shrugged. 'It's listen to me, or listen to Inspector Lestrade. It won't be long before he works out where Mary's got to! I asked around earlier tonight and I learned how close she'd got to Sparrow here — yes, I recognised you, Sparrow!'

he said as Sparrow looked at him in amazement.

'I've been in the game a long time and I know how to find out what I want to know! And however dumb Lestrade is, that young Sergeant Hopkins will soon put two and two together and come looking around here! Now, what's it to be, kids?'

'We'll listen to you, Mr. O'Neill,' said Mary. 'I don't think you mean us any harm.'

So the Pinkerton investigator began to tell them an amazing story. 'First of all, kids,' he said, 'I've been on the look-out for Mary Ashley's stepfather for over a year — long before he met her mother and turned himself into Marvin the Mentalist.'

'Why, what's he done?' said Sparrow.

O'Neill smiled. 'More than you'd believe. Marvin was a member of the worst gang of desperadoes that New York ever saw — and Marvin was one of the worst before he left the Iron Fist gang!'

'He left the gang?' said Wiggins.

'Yeah!' said the American. 'With the

loot — and nobody robs the Iron Fist gang and gets away with it! They've been on the look-out for him ever since!'

'He knew they were coming!' said Mary. 'He was scared, I'm sure he was!'

'He had every reason to be terrified,' said O'Neill. 'He made off — with the loot — over a couple of million dollars' worth of jewels. He knew that when they caught up with him, his life wouldn't be worth a bent nickel.'

'Yet you found him, Mr. O'Neill,' said Mary. 'Wasn't it your duty to arrest him right away?'

'No,' said O'Neill. 'I've been hired to get the jewels back. We want to see the rest of the gang behind bars, but most of all the Pinkerton Agency wants the loot — and I'm not quitting yet!'

The Baker Street Boys listened in utter fascination as O'Neill told of his investigations. He had found Marvin's trail in New York only a few weeks before his appearance at the music hall. And when finally O'Neill crossed the Atlantic to check up on one slender lead, he realised that he had found the treacherous member of the Iron Fist gang.

It had been an almost unbelievable discovery, for who would have thought that the most wanted criminal in the United States would have the nerve to appear in public on the stage? But, so O'Neill explained, when Marvin had met and married Mary's mother, he had looked quite different from The Amazing Marvin the Mentalist.

He had been heavier then, and he wore a beard and a heavy moustache. Now, much lighter and clean-shaven, he had shown the bravado that had made him such a desperate and successful criminal.

'He sure had gall,' said O'Neill. 'But he fooled the gang — none of them picked up his trail.'

'But surely they did!' put in Mary.

'Yeah!' said Wiggins. 'And they killed him!'

O'Neill shook his head. 'I've been on the look-out for the past week,' he said. 'If any of the gang had been around, I'd have spotted them. That's what I've been waiting for: some of them to show up and get Marvin scared so he would panic. But someone else got to him first.'

Wiggins breathed out slowly.

''Strewth!' he said. 'If the gang didn't get him — then who did? And where's the loot?'

'I've got a clue,' said O'Neill. 'I have proof that Mary's stepfather placed his stolen loot in a safety-deposit box in a New York bank. We don't know which bank, but we know that somewhere amongst Marvin's possessions there must be a ticket of some kind that gives him access to his loot. If we can find the secret of the ticket, I can recover the jewels!'

'Marvin's secret,' whispered Sparrow. 'That's what it was.'

Wiggins and the others looked at Sparrow in amazement, for he was staring at Mary as though she was a ghost.

'What's the trouble, kid?' asked O'Neill.

'Sparrow, tell me!' gasped Mary.

'Come on!' growled Wiggins.

'All right — I will!'' cried Sparrow. 'Mary's got the secret of the loot — that's why he was hypnotising her! I saw him do it with her locket — he put her in a trance and said she was never to tell his secret!'

And then Sparrow reached out to touch the silver locket at Mary's neck.

'What is it, Sparrow?' whispered Mary.

'The locket?' said O'Neill.

Wiggins nodded slowly. 'It has to be, doesn't it — let's have a look in that locket of yours, Mary.'

And it was there.

Mary wept when she saw the picture of her dead mother; but when she saw that Marvin had hidden the safety-deposit box ticket behind the picture, she became furious.

'He used me just as he used my poor mother!' she cried. 'He could have had me killed too!'

'Marvin sure was smart,' agreed O'Neill. 'When he figured the gang was after him, he made sure they couldn't get to the loot.'

'He knew I'd take care of the locket!' Mary sobbed. 'It's the only one of my mother's possessions he let me keep!'

Wiggins looked at the ticket for which Marvin had been killed. For a few moments he stood deep in thought, and then suddenly he looked up at the picture on the wall, at the stern features of Mr. Sherlock Holmes.

The Baker Street Boys noticed his abstraction; and so did O'Neill. 'Something bothering you, kid?' he said.

'Oh yes,' said Wiggins. 'Quite a few things as a matter of fact. Things like who gave the blood-spot to Marvin, for a start, and where Queenie is for another. There again, we've got to think about this here ticket and how to catch a murderer, ain't we?'

'Yeh!' said Sparrow. 'What you thinking, Wiggins?'

Wiggins pointed to the picture of Mr. Holmes.

'I was thinking of what Mr. Holmes would do.'

'And what's that?' said Rosie.

'Yeah, kid,' said O'Neill. 'This case isn't finished yet — we want Queenie back and the way to do that is to find the murderer. You got a plan, kid?'

'Sort of,' said Wiggins. 'I'm going to see Dr. Watson to ask him to send a telegram to Mr. Holmes, but meanwhile we'll need

Inspector Lestrade's help.'

'Lestrade!' said Sparrow. 'But he won't have us near him!'

'He will when we take Mary to him,' said Wiggins.

'You're not taking Mary!' cried Rose. 'He thinks she helped the murderer!'

'True,' said Wiggins. 'But Mr. O'Neill and me might persuade him different.'

'How?' said O'Neill. Wiggins looked smug.

'I don't know much about America,' he told O'Neill, 'but I did hear how they catch wolves out there.'

'Wolves, kid?'

'Yeh,' said Wiggins. 'They put out wolf-bait.'

He showed O'Neill and the fascinated Baker Street Boys the ticket. Then he slipped it back into the locket and fastened the locket around Mary's neck.

'What are you doing that for?' whispered Mary.

O'Neill understood:

'Wolf-bait!'

* * *

Queenie struggled for hours in the dingy box room; at one time, she thought the cords at her wrists had given a little, but before she could be sure, exhaustion overtook her.

As the cold grey light of another dawn filtered into the boxroom, Queenie slept.

Her dreams were full of terror.

6

'What!' cried Inspector Lestrade to me when he first heard early the next morning that the Baker Street Boys were again involved.

'Amateurs again? I won't have it, Hopkins! No ragamuffin amateurs are going to impede this investigation! It's bad enough having a wretched American investigator up to his neck in gangsters and stolen jewels poking about here, but I will not have those would-be sleuths near me! Get a statement from each of them, Hopkins, and see if you can find something to charge them with.'

I told my superior that it wasn't likely that I could.

'Charge them with abducting the girl — what's her name?'

'Mary Ashley, sir. But they didn't abduct her, from what I understand of the situation. Wiggins — '

'Don't speak to me about Wiggins! Mr.

Holmes might hold him in high regard, but so far as I'm concerned he's just another meddling urchin!'

It had seemed an easy business at first. There was the dead gangster (as we found him to be once O'Neill reported to us) stretched out on his dressing room floor with a knife through his heart; but Maccarelli the knife-thrower could prove that he had been drinking in company at the time of the murder.

One by one, everyone who had access to the backstage area produced an alibi of sorts. Not every alibi was perfect — a dozen different people could have slipped into the star's dressing room and knifed him in a moment. But who had actually done it?

'One of these desperadoes,' said Inspector Lestrade. 'O'Neill told us they're a murderous bunch wanting their revenge on Marvin.'

But O'Neill had also told us that he didn't believe the Iron Fist gang had located Marvin. So we were thrown back again into looking for the murderer amongst the music hall people; and worse still, from

Lestrade's point of view, we were forced to listen to a gang of amateurs who claimed to be able to solve the case!

'Oh, send them in!' declared my boss. 'I've listened to O'Neill, so I might as well hear what Wiggins has got to say.'

I did point out that, but for Sparrow's resourcefulness, Mary Ashley might also be dead with a knife-thrust through her heart; but Inspector Lestrade snorted angrily:

'This isn't an investigation, it's chaos!'

And when he heard the American and the Baker Street Boys outlining their plan he gasped:

'It isn't chaos — it's lunacy! What, wolf-bait? Wolf-bait! And you, Miss Ashley, have agreed to be the bait? Why, it's plain lunacy!'

It was not as lunatic a proposal as it seemed, and eventually Inspector Lestrade agreed to it. Wolf-bait was as good a way of describing Wiggins' scheme as any — but Mary Ashley was the bait, and the unknown knife-wielder was our quarry.

It was an audacious scheme. Quite simply, we were going to put Mary back on the stage of the music hall.

She would take part in the act she knew so well, and we hoped that the murderer would make an attempt to find the secret he had already killed once for.

'It sure is a crafty kind of plan,' said O'Neill in the stunned silence that followed Wiggins' and Sparrow's explanations.

'Crafty isn't what I'd call it,' said Inspector Lestrade sourly. 'And who's to be the new Marvin, always supposing I agree to this imbecile scheme?'

Wiggins grinned. 'In a posh suit — me!'

'Wiggins knows the act, Inspector,' said Sparrow. 'And there'd be crowds wanting to see Mary now her old man's been knifed — it'll be sensational!'

'And it will bring the murderer out of hiding, Inspector,' said O'Neill. 'We'll let it be known that Mary has inherited something of great value. It's bound to attract the murderer.'

'Course!' declared Sparrow. 'It's as plain as the nose on your face!' Which was an unfortunate thing to say, for Inspector

Lestrade's nose was large and red. Inspector Lestrade glared back at Sparrow; but the more he heard, the more he was convinced, and so it was that the following day's newspapers were full of the revival of Marvin's popular act — minus the murdered Marvin, but with a mysterious hypnotist called Arnold Wiggins.

And, of course, Mary Ashley!

* * *

People flocked to the opening night.

What made it more attractive for them was the promise that all the acts which had performed on the night of the murder of Marvin would again be assembled. Crowds clamoured to get into Trump's music hall, for what greater thrill could there be than to see the orphaned Mary in the music-hall where there had been such a gruesome murder?

'Full house!' said Mr. Trump to Bert. 'Excellent!'

'Sparrow!' called Bert. 'Placards for Signor Macaroni!'

'Maccarelli!' yelled the knife-thrower.

'Don't make bad jokes about me, or maybe I stick a knife in you, Bert!'

'Did you hear that, Hopkins?' demanded Lestrade, who was with me backstage. 'A threat!'

'Macaroni wouldn't harm a fly!' said Sparrow.

'Hush!' said Rosie. 'Keep a good look out!'

'Quite,' said Lestrade, so we settled back in our dusty hiding-place amongst rolls of painted canvas and miscellaneous stage-furniture whilst knives were thrown, the songs were sung and the rest of the show was performed — until, at last, with a roll of drums and a crash of cymbals, Arnold Wiggins, The Boy Hypnotist in a borrowed suit, and Mary Ashley appeared.

How the audience loved it!

They gasped and cheered; they clapped and stamped their feet; they shouted and struggled to become one of those chosen to take the stage and have a ring, or a watch, or a wallet identified. Wiggins turned out to be a most competent stand-in, too.

He hadn't had the training or the stage presence of Marvin, of course; but his confident bearing dominated the audience, and his loud voice made him a passable stage hypnotist.

I was quite enjoying the show, but Lestrade had become very impatient.

'Wolf-bait!' he growled. 'Hypnotism! Amateur sleuths!' But the amateur was doing very well on stage.

'Now, Mary!' he called. 'You can't see a blooming thing, can you?'

'No, Master!' said Mary.

'And you don't know what's in my hand, do you? She don't,' he told the audience. 'Not yet, 'cos she can't read my mind yet!'

The audience yelled for him to read Mary's mind, so Wiggins grinned and went on:

'Concentrate, Mary, my dear! Wipe your mind clear and concentrate! Are you ready?'

'Yes, Master . . . I see . . . I believe it is a handkerchief!'

Howls of approval greeted Mary's words. The audience cheered on and demanded more, and it was an exhausted — but exhilarated — Wiggins and Mary that finally left the stage.

'And still no sign of the murderer!' growled Lestrade.

'He's not shown his hand yet, sir,' I answered. 'But he couldn't tackle Mary on stage could he? Oh, by the way, sir, I've just heard that we have two distinguished visitors in the audience!'

'Not the Prince of Wales!' gasped Lestrade. 'Trump told me that he's been expecting royalty to see the act!'

'No, sir. It's Mr. Sherlock Holmes and Dr. Watson — they're in a box at the back of the hall.'

'As if I didn't have enough amateurs back-stage!' Lestrade muttered. 'We've got to do something to make that murderer reveal himself! But how?'

We were completely at a loss.

We had no way of knowing that poor brave Queenie was just struggling free of her bonds; nor that one of those unexpected turns of fortune which are the downfall of so many villains was even now occurring.

* * *

'I'm glad that's over!' sighed Mary, as she reached the fatal dressing room. 'And I never want to see this place after tonight.'

'But we've not seen the murderer yet — or at least he ain't tried to grab you,' said Wiggins. 'And Queenie — where's she?'

Mary put her hand instinctively to the locket.

'Poor Queenie — I'd give all the jewels to have her back! But I don't want this locket with me anymore! I'm scared, Wiggins!'

'Scared, who's scared?' called Mr. Trump from the doorway. 'Can I be of any assistance?'

Mary gave a sigh of relief. 'Please put this away in your safe, Mr. Trump — I daren't go around in it any longer.'

Mr. Trump took the locket. 'But of course, Mary — hello, what's that noise?'

Heavy boots pounded in the corridor, and a burly police-constable rushed by. He ignored Mr. Trump and headed for Inspector Lestrade.

'Sir — we've spotted him!' he called. 'A big, nasty thug, just got in!'

'Trouble?' said Mr. Trump. 'I'll put this

locket away and come up front.'

Wiggins and Mary ran to find the others, who were all together on the deserted stage. Everyone milled around trying to find out what was happening, and when the news spread that a thug was loose, there was panic. And then came the sound of a scream.

'Mary!' gasped Sparrow. 'That's her!'

'Where?' I snapped.

'Trump's office!' Sparrow shouted back.

'She was here — a second ago!' Wiggins cried; but already he and Sparrow were pushing their way through the yelling crowd. I followed as fast as I could, but one after another of the artistes got in my way.

'Is it another murder?' cried Madame Pompadour.

'I don't know — let me loose!' I yelled back, and I could hear Inspector Lestrade trying to break free of Signor Maccarelli, who was yelling something about his knives.

'Chaos!' yelled Lestrade. 'Chaos!'

I reached the office a few seconds after Wiggins and Sparrow. Mary was safe, but her attacker was dead.

He lay on the floor with a knife in his back — just like Marvin.

'There!' Wiggins said, holding the terrified girl. 'It's all right, he can't harm you now!'

And he could not. He was a big, powerfully built thug with an ugly face and the hands of a prize-fighter. In one of his hands was a silver chain — but no locket!

'Ah!' cried Lestrade. 'We've got him!'

'We ain't,' said Sparrow. 'We've got the one that handed Marvin the note with the blood-spot. I recognise him!'

'Yes,' said Wiggins. 'We've got the bloke that worked for the murderer, himself — and here's Queenie!' he yelled as Queenie rushed into the room.

'Mary!' she cried.

'Oh, Queenie, you're back!' gasped Mary, and the two girls rushed into one another's arms.

But Queenie detected something that we had missed.

'Chloroform!' she cried. 'He's the one that grabbed me! I can smell it!'

I opened the dead man's other hand

and found a chloroform pad.

'So we've got the accomplice,' said Lestrade. 'But not the murderer.'

O'Neill entered the office.

'And the murderer's got Mary's locket,' he said. 'Not that that's going to help him — we weren't foolish enough to leave the deposit box ticket in it.'

'But who is he?' growled Lestrade. 'Queenie — did you see anyone, apart from this brute?'

'No! I was in the other room — I only got a glimpse of this horrible bloke, and the other one kept well out of sight,' she said. 'And he kept his voice down too.'

'But surely you'd recognise something about him?' I said. 'Anything!' cried Wiggins. 'We've got to find him Queenie, or Mary's always going to be in danger!'

Queenie shook her head hopelessly.

'I was lying there for hours trying to identify him. I can't think of anything! Except . . . '

'Yes?' cried Lestrade.

'Think, please, Queenie!' sobbed Mary. 'I can't live with this hanging over me.'

'I've got it!' cried Queenie, and she

held her hand up for silence. 'Listen!'

There was a slight metallic clicking sound from outside. Queenie pointed to the door.

'That's what I heard!'

'What is it?' cried Lestrade, as Sparrow flung himself through the door, followed by Wiggins, Beaver, Shiner, and myself — in that order.

'Trump!' cried Sparrow, as he darted after the owner of Trump's Music hall. 'He always clicks his heels like that — get him!'

It all began so quickly that the police-constables were bewildered; and only the Baker Street Boys were fast enough to spot him.

Trump knew his own theatre better than anyone. He fled into the deep gloom and was lost from sight until Sparrow spotted him.

'There he goes!' he yelled. 'See, he's making for that balcony — there's an exit to the roof! We'll never find him if he gets up there!'

Trump leapt for a trapeze. He turned and grinned savagely at his pursuers; he knew he had only to swing up on to the balcony to be free.

Then Wiggins spotted someone above him: 'It's up to you, sir!' he yelled.

'Who's up there?' cried Lestrade. Queenie laughed. 'Mr. Holmes!'

At that moment, Mr. Sherlock Holmes leant forward and slashed the ropes; and the heavy bulk of the murderer crashed to the stage!

Dr. Watson peered down. 'Ah, Lestrade,' he said. 'I see you've got your man?'

'Damnation!' hissed Lestrade.

'Maybe we should offer our thanks to Mr. Holmes,' I suggested. 'It would be tactful, sir?'

'Yes, yes!' conceded Lestrade. 'Many thanks, Mr. Holmes, sir!'

'And to Queenie?'

'If I must!'

'And the rest of the Baker Street Boys, sir?'

Lestrade forced himself to make a speech of congratulations and thanks, in which the artistes and stagehands joined. O'Neill came forward to thank Mr. Holmes and the Boys on behalf of his clients, and also to make sure that Mary — and Queenie — were recovering from their ordeal.

Later, the American talked to them about the case — and Mary Ashley's future.

'I guess that wraps it up,' he said. 'Mary's going back to the States. I'm going to collect the loot. The mystery's finished and the case is solved. I had a few words with Mr. Holmes before I came here and he said that Wiggins was right to call him in, though he's sorry he came so late. I guess you know that he's still trying to find Moriarty?'

'Of course,' said Wiggins. 'But Mr. Holmes came at the right time, didn't he?'

'Just like the Baker Street Boys,' said O'Neill.

'Ah,' said Wiggins. 'We have our methods.'

The Disappearing Despatch Case

1

I had been recording the exploits of the Baker Street Irregulars, which is how Mr. Sherlock Holmes referred to the gang of street urchins he occasionally employed, for only a few months when one of their most hazardous adventures took place.

I have called it the case of the Missing Despatch Case, though Sparrow suggested that a better title would be 'Things ain't always what they seems'. He should know, since he was present at the start of the adventure.

There is no doubt that Mr. Holmes would have taken over the case had he not been desperately ill; but he had just been seriously wounded by the evil Professor Moriarty, and the poison from Moriarty's sword-stick still ran in his veins.

He was able to help in the affair when it seemed that the bizarre mystery would never be solved, however, though as Mr.

Holmes said later the entire credit must lie with the Baker Street Irregulars for its successful outcome.

It all began one vile midwinter evening at a time when most of the shops had put up their shutters and the only people to be seen in the thick, yellow fog were either hurrying home to a fireside, or trying to earn a few pence.

Even those few had had enough of the raw, dank, chilly fog.

'Let's pack up, Rosie,' Shiner called. 'Look at me hands. They're dropping off. There ain't no one wanting shoe-shines, not at this time of night. Let's pack up.'

'Here,' said Rosie, who was no bigger than Shiner. They were both small, undernourished children of about twelve years of age, wearing all the clothes they possessed. Rosie held a couple of hot chestnuts in her ragged mitt.

'What's that?' shivered Shiner.

'Hot and good,' said Rosie. 'Got them from the hot chestnut man up the street. One each.'

'It's hot!' yelled Shiner, juggling the chestnut from hand to hand.

'What did I tell you?' said Rosie, grinning at him.

'Ain't it just come off the stove?'

Shiner stopped his complaints as he heard footsteps a few yards away. He slipped the hot chestnut into his pocket and seized the tools of his trade.

'Shoe-shine, sir?' he called, as a distinguished-looking elderly gentleman came into view through the swirling fog. 'Do you a good one, best in London for tuppence.'

The man hesitated as he saw Shiner and Rosie, and the two children saw he had a look of compassion on his face.

'Loverly flowers, sir?' said Rosie, trying to smile in spite of the freezing fog that chapped her lips and rasped in her throat. 'Only tuppence a bunch, sir.'

Shiner held his breath. He had been out on the streets since before dawn, and all day he had taken only seven pence. Rosie's stock of flowers was still almost untouched, since she had not been able to afford the best and freshest blooms in Covent Garden that morning, and it was a sad-looking display of wilted flowers that she offered so hopefully to the customer.

But her smile was perfection.

'Here's threepence,' said the elderly gentleman, taking the bunch she offered. 'Keep the penny change for that smile of yours, my dear. I won't wait for a shoe-shine,' he added to Shiner, 'but I'll remember your face when I come this way again, boy.'

He went on his way smiling, leaving Rosie looking at the silver threepenny piece and Shiner packing up his brushes.

'I ain't got a lovely smile, Rosie,' he said, 'but never mind. Threepence is threepence, and that's enough for one night — Here!' he yelled as someone charged into them, sending them flying.

'My thrupenny — where's it gone?' cried Rosie.

'Who was that? Clumsy great bloke!'

A big figure vanished into the mist and the two children yelled until the sound of his heavy footsteps was lost in the fog. They scrabbled about searching for the silver coin, which had been sent spinning from Rosie's hand. Neither of them had seen where it had fallen.

They were still peering at the ground when two more of the Baker Street Boys joined them. They were Beaver, a biggish boy of about fourteen, and Sparrow, who at eleven or so had much in common with the quick-witted town-bird he had been named after.

'What have you lost?' called Sparrow. 'Dropped your diamonds, have you, Rosie?' he asked her, though Rosie ignored him.

Beaver dumped the pile of newspapers he had been carrying. 'What we looking for, Rosie?' he too asked.

'A thrupenny piece,' said Rosie. 'A big bloke with a stick in his hand just knocked me and Shiner flying.'

'I saw him,' said Sparrow. 'Six-foot and more, and a big red beard. He looked as though he was after something going along like the clappers, he was. He wasn't the one what gave you the thrupenny, was he?'

'Don't be daft,' said Shiner. 'He's the kind what'd give you a crack with his stick, that's all. Found it!' he cried.

Beaver inspected the threepenny piece.

'Got it from an old fellow,' said Rosie. 'He gave me the penny extra 'cos I smiled at him — he said I'd got a loverly smile. Then he walks off grinning to himself. A toff, he is.'

'I saw him too,' said Beaver. 'Tall and thin, that him?'

'Yeh,' said Sparrow. 'He was carrying a little case, wasn't he? I saw him go off into a tobacconist's at the end of Baker Street — old Merriman's, who buys a paper off of us.'

'How about the big bloke with the stick?' said Shiner. 'Where did he get to?'

'Sparrow saw him, not me,' said Beaver.

'Why?' asked Sparrow, grinning at Shiner. 'You going to give him a piece of your mind for knocking into you? I'd say he's big enough to put you into his pocket, and your brushes too, Shiner!'

The dispute might have gone on a little longer if Rosie hadn't stopped it by walking off into the fog saying that she had heard enough and she was hungry, and if some smart alecks wanted to stand around the street arguing, that was their look-out. But she, Rosie, was going home.

She hadn't been walking for long when the others joined her, and no sooner had they caught up with her than the incident occurred which was to set off the whole series of events of the Disappearing Despatch Case. It began with a cry from the direction of Merriman's shop.

'Oh, do help me someone!' quavered what sounded like an old woman's voice. 'Help!'

'Here!' called Beaver, who was ahead of the others. 'Come on!' They all ran after him, with Shiner and Rosie struggling with their belongings towards the sounds of a fierce struggle and more terrified calls for help.

'Hold on!' yelled Sparrow. 'We're coming!'

Beaver and Sparrow arrived simultaneously at the source of the cries, and they were in time to see what happened. Outside Merriman's shop, a struggle was taking place.

'It's him with the red beard!' yelled Sparrow to Rosie and Shiner. The big man was struggling with an old woman who was trying to keep possession of a shopping-basket by flailing with her umbrella at him.

As he grabbed at the basket, she countered with a blow at his face, but he gave a snarling cry and then he had her by one huge hand around the throat.

'Get him!' yelled Sparrow, pushing the larger boy forward.

Beaver rushed towards the man with his fists raised, but already help was on the way. From inside the well-lit tobacconist's shop, a tall figure emerged, blinking against the sudden gloom of the drifting yellow fog but quickly grasping what was happening.

In a loud and commanding voice, the elderly gentleman who had given the threepenny piece to Rosie called out:

'Why, you villain — leave her alone! Merriman, sound your whistle for the police!'

And without any further reflection he dropped his parcels and despatch case and raised his silver-mounted cane as he approached the burly ruffian and his struggling, gasping victim.

Beaver and Sparrow were already engaged, but not for long.

'Knock his legs from under him!' yelled Sparrow to Beaver as they dodged both the umbrella and the burly man's wide, sweeping blows. 'He'll have that poor old lady dead, strangled, so he will — aaaah!'

And Sparrow found himself hurled into the cobbled street as the red-bearded man snarled and caught him with a hard blow to the head. Beaver, too, was unable to give much assistance, for the ruffian could easily handle a terrified old woman and a couple of ragamuffins at the same time. In a moment, he had also knocked Beaver out of the fight, so that when Rosie and Shiner appeared through the gloom the first thing they saw was the two members of the Baker Street Boys struggling to their feet and wailing that they were bleeding to blinking death.

'Now, you villain, try fighting a man!' they heard the distinguished looking elderly man call, and they saw him cut at the attacker's head with his cane.

Had the blow landed, it would have

taken much of the fight out of the robber, but somehow it missed — perhaps by chance, perhaps by a fortunate glance from the poor old woman's umbrella; certainly, it was a powerful and well-aimed blow in true cavalry style. It was, however, ineffective, and worse than that it served to enrage the burly robber even more.

'Yaaargh!' he snarled, turning to face his new adversary, and Rosie quailed as she saw the beetling brows and the wild-eyed stare of the robber, whilst it took all of Shiner's resolution to begin his own attack, hacking at the man's shins.

That too was ineffectual, for before Shiner could attempt to kick the red-bearded man, he had dashed the stick from the elderly gentleman's hand and knocked him to the ground. Shiner saw the attacker scrabble for the cudgel at his belt to finish off the fallen old man, so he pressed home his own attack and kicked him hard on the ankle.

'Teufel!' howled the attacker, shocked by the blow. 'Aaaarh!' he cursed, the cudgel now in his hand, his mad eyes promising revenge and his whole face a mask of such rage that Shiner fled. A loud blast on a whistle stopped him.

It was the call which would summon any nearby police-officer, and the attacker clearly knew its meaning. He looked around him and saw both Beaver and Sparrow on their feet, both with a look of fierce determination on their faces. He looked further and saw that his victim was by no means completely cowed, for she still retained her umbrella in her hand.

And when he glanced towards the tobacconist's shop, he could see that Merriman had taken the opportunity of arming himself with a sturdy truncheon. The odds were too much for him, and without another moment's delay, he turned and ran into the fog, with Merriman's cries ringing after him:

'Stop that man — stop, thief!'

2

Beaver and Sparrow needed no prompting, nor did Shiner now that he was in the company of two of the bigger Baker Street Boys. Heart pounding and lungs aching with the cold, they rushed along the alleyways after the red-bearded villain.

Rosie decided that her place was with Mr. Merriman and the victims of the robber's attack. The old woman was moaning and clutching her neck where she had been grabbed; whilst the distinguished elderly gentleman lay in a pool of blood, glistening in the flickering gaslight.

Mr. Merriman was so agitated that he was unable to decide what should be done.

'You can stop blowing that whistle,' Rosie told him.

'There won't be any coppers around now — they'll all be in the pub up Baker Street. Here, listen to this toff's heart

— is he a goner?'

'A goner?' cried Mr. Merriman, hurrying to where Rosie bent to listen at the elderly gentleman's chest.

'I hope not, indeed I hope not! That's Sir Alfred Connyngham, one of my regulars. Is that blood?'

'Course it's blinking blood,' said Rosie, accustomed to the violence of London's streets. 'And if you don't get a doctor to him soon, he'll be a goner for sure, dead as mutton, that's what.'

'A doctor?' whispered Mr. Merriman. 'Where am I going to find a doctor for him? And look at this poor lady too! She's fainting clean away, what with that brute's hands on her neck. Look at her! I don't know what to do!'

'You take her inside your shop, Mr. Merriman, while I see to this toff here — what did you say his name was?'

Sir Alfred Connyngham groaned just then.

'Whoever he is, he's still wiv us,' Rosie went on, as Mr. Merriman dithered and moaned. 'Go on — get the old girl inside. And just you keep still, your lordship or whatever you are — can you hear me?'

Again Sir Alfred groaned, and Mr. Merriman saw the sense in getting one of the victims off the street.

'You're all right,' Rosie assured the elderly gentleman.

'You've been bashed by a bully, but you'll live, and the old girl's all right too that you tried to help — there, old Merriman's took 'er inside, so stop worrying, will yer?'

Slowly and painfully, the old woman was half-supported into the shop, clutching her shopping-basket, her umbrella and Merriman's arm; however, her dress was askew, and as she passed beside the half-conscious nobleman and Rosie, a handkerchief slipped from her pocket.

'Here,' began Rosie, but the woman didn't hear her, so Rosie dabbed at the wound on Sir Alfred's forehead with it. 'Don't want to hurt you,' she told him, 'but it's a nasty sight — no, don't try to sit up. You've been hit hard — and you don't deserve it, a kind old gent like you.'

'Rosie?' called a familiar voice through the yellow gloom. 'You there, Rosie?'

'Yeh — and you can get busy, Sparrer,' called Rosie back, as first Sparrow, then Beaver and finally Shiner puffed and panted into view.

'Lost him!' cried Shiner. 'We was right up to him and he just vanished!'

'Like magic, it was,' agreed Sparrow. 'Beaver nearly had him by his coat-tails when — '

'When you lost him, and that'll do for now about him,' said Rosie. 'We'll see to this gentleman now he's coming round a bit — Sparrer, you hop it and fetch Dr. Watson smart now — go on!' she cried, and Sparrow ran off without argument, which was unusual for him, while Beaver and Shiner helped prop up Sir Alfred.

'Can we get him inside?' said Beaver. 'It's miserable cold out here. You ready to move, sir?' he asked the semiconscious nobleman.

'Where's Mr. Merriman, Rosie?'

'He's in too much of a dither to help,' she told Beaver. 'Let's get you up, sir,' she said to Sir Alfred.

'Beaver's right — you'll freeze out here. What's that?' she went on, hearing a faint inquiry from the injured man. 'The old girl, you say?'

'Poor lady — what happened to her?' whispered Sir Alfred, who was slowly recovering his senses.

'Don't trouble yourself, Sir Alfred!' called Merriman, who reappeared from inside his shop. 'I've settled her into the snug before a fire, and she's taken care of. But we must see to you, Your Lordship — here, give a hand, will you?' he said to Beaver and Shiner. 'This is Sir Alfred Connyngham, you know, a member of the Government!'

'Is he, now?' said Shiner, who was deeply impressed by the news. 'Easy, Your Lordship!' cried Merriman, who had managed to control his initial panicky reaction. 'The police will be here before long — and a doctor! Did you send for a doctor, girl?' he asked Rosie.

'Course I did,' said Rosie. 'Dr. Watson from Baker Street!'

'Ah, of course!' said Merriman. 'Why didn't I think of him?' There was a groan from the injured nobleman then.

'Give a hand here!' ordered Merriman.

'Lean on me, sir,' said Beaver, offering a solid shoulder to the tottering man, and slowly they walked through the dense fog towards the shop.

They were able to see the brightly-lit shop-window as a hazy beacon in the gloom; and just as the two boys and Merriman —and Rosie, adding her wiry strength — supported Sir Alfred towards the open door, a member of the London police answered Merriman's urgent summons.

'Who blew that whistle?' demanded PC Boot, clattering towards them. 'Here, what's happening — Mr. Merriman, who's these here ragamuffins?'

'Good Samaritans, all of them!' answered Merriman sharply. 'You took your time, my man, for I blew I don't know how many times on my whistle — where were you, Boot? This is your beat, isn't it?'

Boot began to apologise for the delay when Merriman found another subject for his nervous anger.

This time it was a short, slim-built middle-aged man with bushy side-whiskers and a plaid cape and hat, who was clutching a large holdall of the kind termed a carpet-bag, and, to Merriman at least, he seemed to be an intrusion on the scene, for the tobacconist said:

'I'm sorry, sir, I have not a moment to spare for you — not a single moment, sir! I can't serve you, no matter who you may be, for Sir Alfred needs my attention!'

The man turned and left and the mystery took another turn, for Sir Alfred was then reminded of his own possessions.

'Merriman!' he cried, suddenly recovering. And then he recognised the presence of a policeman too.

'Constable?' he said, puzzled momentarily. 'I was attacked — yes! I had my despatch case — Do you have it, Officer?'

'Me, sir? I only just arrived this instant, sir, and I'm afraid I know nothing of — '

Once more, Boot was cut short, for with a loud cry Sir Alfred Connyngham realised the extent of his loss.

'Let me go!' he cried to the two boys and to Merriman. 'Who's this? Why, it's the flower-girl. Yes, you helped me, I recall it now. My things — where are they?'

'Here's your stick, sir,' said Shiner. 'And your tobacco parcel from the smell of it — and here's the flowers, not much to say for them, I'm afraid — '

'But my despatch case!' cried Sir Alfred. 'It's black, and it has the insignia of the Crown. It must be here,' he said, staggering and almost falling to the ground once more.

PC Boot might have been slow in arriving, and he certainly had been slow-witted in allowing himself to be criticised by the tobacconist, but at the mention of official matters he immediately understood his duty.

'I believe I am addressing Sir Alfred Connyngham, am I right, Your Lordship?' he said, and he put one burly arm below the nobleman's elbow and helped him towards the shop.

'Yes,' mumbled Sir Alfred. 'Indeed you are, Officer,' he went on as he struggled to remain conscious. 'You must find my despatch case immediately! It contains important Government papers — '

He did not finish his remarks as he blacked out once more, and Boot had to take the whole of his weight. Boot settled the nobleman into the shop and addressed Merriman briskly, for at the mention of Sir Alfred's loss he immediately understood his duty.

'You look after His Lordship,' he said to the tobacconist. 'You,' he told Beaver, 'get yourself up the road to the police station as if seven devils was after you — bring the Duty Officer and some men, and say Sir Alfred Connyngham's hurt — hop it! And you two,' he told Rosie and Shiner, 'you two help me look for this case.'

Beaver ran off as he was told. The evening had begun with a fight, which in itself was exciting enough, followed by a chase that had resulted in a mystery. And now he was acting on behalf of a Government Minister — it was almost as good as being employed by Mr. Holmes himself!

Rosie and Shiner were less happy.

'It's gone,' said Rosie, after she and Shiner and PC Boot had searched every inch of the area.

'It can't have,' said Boot. 'Are you two sure he had it with him? I mean, the poor gentleman isn't feeling quite himself just now, what with the crack he had.'

But Rosie was sure that Sir Alfred had had the despatch case when he bought the flowers from her; she recalled seeing him hitch it under his arm when he reached for his pocket to pay her.

Boot looked unhappy too as they returned to Merriman's shop. 'This,' he said, 'will be a bad business. It has all the hallmarks — here, that's Dr. Watson in with Sir Alfred, ain't it?'

'Yeh,' said Shiner. 'Now if he'd got Mr. Sherlock Holmes wiv him we wouldn't be in such a tizzy. But he's not here, or he'd have it all puzzled out in half a tick.'

'Maybe he would, and maybe he wouldn't,' said Boot, entering the shop. 'But this is a job for a professional. Now, keep back and hush. Evening, sir,' he said to Dr. Watson.

Dr. Watson looked up and grunted as he finished inserting a stitch into a long wound on the unconscious nobleman's forehead.

'PC Boot at your service,' went on the constable. 'It's a nasty business. Matter of an attack on an old woman and Sir Alfred Connyngham intervening on her behalf and losing his important State documents, sir.'

Dr. Watson looked up and nodded to the Baker Street Boys, who kept discreetly in the background, their eyes shining with excited interest.

'I heard from Sparrow what had happened, or part of it anyway,' he said. 'It was smart of him to think of me — Sir Alfred needed instant attention. Merriman told me a little too, but so far no one's mentioned an old lady. I know about a red-bearded brute who can walk through brick walls, and I know from Sir Alfred's ramblings that some extremely important documents were contained in his despatch case, but what's this about an old lady being injured? I should look at her too — good grief, Merriman, what's the matter with you?' he demanded, for the tobacconist was acting in a strange manner.

'Where is she?' the tobacconist was bleating, as he pointed to the inner room he used as a snug.

It was a small room, with one tiny window and no outside door. And it was obvious to all those who could see inside that it was quite empty.

'Where is who?' snapped Dr. Watson.

'The old girl,' said Shiner.

'What was being strangled,' added Rosie.

'What Merriman brought in here, sir,' finished PC Boot.

'The old lady who was the subject of the red-bearded brute's attack?' said Dr. Watson.

'Yes, Doctor,' said Merriman, who had recovered his wits by now. 'Didn't you see her come out, sir?' Boot asked Dr. Watson.

'No, my man, I didn't. Merriman too will tell you that no one passed through his shop from the time I arrived to attend to Sir Alfred,' Dr. Watson told him.

'And I'd have seen her from down the street if she'd gone while we were searching for the despatch case,' said Boot.

'And us,' said Shiner.

'That's another one what's disappeared,' said Sparrow. 'Just like magic.'

'Only nastier,' said Rosie.

Just then, Boot heard the clatter of a hansom arriving, followed by loud calls from a commanding voice.

PC Boot turned pale, but he tried to sound reassuring.

'I hear Inspector Lestrade calling,' he said. 'Excuse me, sir, I'm sure we'll have the villain arrested shortly and the rest of this business cleared up.'

With that, he left to greet Inspector Lestrade.

'Lestrade?' grunted Dr. Watson. 'I fear it will take more than Inspector Lestrade's brains to puzzle out tonight's mystery.'

3

'Then what happened?' said Wiggins.

Rosie and Shiner, together with Beaver and Sparrow, were wolfing down the Irish stew that Queenie had made from a four-pennyworth of scrag end of mutton and some vegetables she had picked up from the litter around the stalls at Covent Garden that morning.

Wiggins felt slightly peeved that this was his first news of the night's adventure since, at fifteen, he was the oldest of the street urchins who lived in the cellar of the derelict house near Baker Street.

He looked up at the framed picture of Sherlock Holmes and told himself that patience was one of the Master's qualities; but the effect of his warning to himself didn't last long.

'Can't you stop eating for a minute and talk?' he demanded.

'I likes my stew hot,' announced Sparrow.

'Queenie's stew's too good not to eat

hot!' agreed Shiner.

'I'll tell you,' said Beaver, mopping his plate with a crust. 'Inspector Lestrade told us to hop it and let him get on wiv the case.'

'That's right,' agreed Rosie. 'Hopkins,' he says, 'get a statement from those raga-muffins and clear them out of my way. There's important State documents gone missing, and I can't be interrupted by a crew of would-be child-detectives.' That's what he says to Sergeant Hopkins.'

Rosie had reported Lestrade's words with great faithfulness, and you may as well know how I knew. It is here that I, Sergeant Hopkins, must reveal myself. Just as Dr. Watson recorded the exploits of Mr. Holmes, so I have attempted to leave a record of those adventures and incidents in which the great man was involved only to a limited extent; I mean, of course, the activities of the Baker Street Irregulars, who at the time I speak of were being questioned by their leader, Arnold Wiggins.

'He called us what?' demanded Wiggins of Rosie.

‘‘Would-be detectives?’’

‘That’s what he said,’ agreed Sparrow.

‘Cheek!’ growled Wiggins. ‘Why, Mr. Holmes said to us only a few weeks back that we’re more use than a dozen of the bobbies, each one of us! As for Lestrade, he wouldn’t know a clue if it bit his ankle for him.’

‘And he said to Merriman he was glad Mr. Holmes wasn’t around too,’ announced Beaver.

‘Did he tell you that in the cab?’ said Wiggins, who was practically fuming by this time.

‘In the cab!’ laughed Beaver. ‘He didn’t take me along in the hansom — I ran alongside. No, I heard him say to Hopkins and Merriman that it wasn’t a case for amateurs like Mr. Holmes and us.’

Wiggins and Queenie gasped with rage.

‘And what did Dr. Watson say about that?’ asked Queenie.

But Lestrade had been more circumspect than to allow his remarks to be overheard by Dr. Watson, as I can confirm. Inspector Lestrade had his faults, but he would never wittingly offend a man of influence — he kept his criticisms of Mr. Holmes and the Irregulars to his subordinates, myself and the unfortunate PC Boot, and to Merriman. Poor Boot came in for an ear-shaking tirade immediately afterwards, but that was Lestrade's way — he would bully his inferiors whilst sucking up to his superiors.

'Amateurs!' fumed Wiggins. 'We're not amateurs — if Mr. Holmes was here we could have this case solved in a jiffy!'

'But he ain't,' pointed out Shiner. 'Poor Mr. Holmes is near death's door, after he got stabbed by Moriarty.'

'So he is,' said Wiggins, and he stared at the picture of the world's foremost detective for so long that the others began to feel restless.

'What are you staring like that for?' said Rosie. 'You're making me feel all unnecessary, Wiggins.'

'I was thinking,' said Wiggins, 'that Mr. Holmes is in that clinic in Switzerland, ain't he?'

'Yeh?' said Shiner.

'Yeh,' said Wiggins. 'And we're here.'

Queenie sighed. 'And we know what

Wiggins means, don't we?' she said to the others.

'Elementary, my dear Queenie,' said Wiggins.

'We're going to show Inspector Lestrade he's wrong. We're going to solve the case of the missing documents — here, what's that?' he said, as Rosie slowly drew out the handkerchief which had been dropped by the old lady at the scene of the attack.

Sparrow took it from her. 'Urgghh! Blood!' he said.

'Sir Alfred's blood, that's what,' agreed Rosie. 'I mopped him up wiv it — I couldn't give it back to the old girl, not when she'd done a bunk, could I?'

Wiggins pointed to a monogram which had been partially concealed by the congealed blood.

'That's an 'O',' he said. 'Anyway, it's not a ladies' handkerchief, it's too big. What's 'O' for?'

''Orace,' said Shiner. ''Orrible 'Orace,' Rosie said.

' 'Orrible 'Orace from 'Ounslow,' Sparrow went on. 'It's a clue, Wiggins!'

'It might be,' said Wiggins, who was getting ready to go out into the cold night. 'But just now I'm going off to do what he'd do,' he said, indicating the picture of Sherlock Holmes.

Queenie, Shiner and Beaver also decided to go with Wiggins, but Rosie said she was too tired to face the icy fog and Sparrow had his own plans.

'Not coming, Sparrer?' Beaver asked him.

'Nah,' said Sparrow, but he didn't elaborate, so the four others left him behind with Rosie.

'How about you?' yawned Rosie as she saw that Sparrow was putting on his coat and ragged cloth cap.

Sparrow lifted the silken handkerchief from the table.

'See this, Rosie girl,' he said, slipping his hand into the silk, which parted to reveal a pocket.

'Funny kind of handkerchief,' agreed Rosie.

'I've seen one like it once,' Sparrow told her. 'Down at the Alhambra.'

'What? Down at the music hall? Did

some toff have it?'

'Nah,' said Sparrow. 'Some magician. And I'm going to ask about him.'

''Orrible 'Orace from 'Ounslow?' said Rosie, but Sparrow had slid out of the door into the yellow fog.

'Magic again,' she said, settling beside the fire. 'Nasty magic too — I hope Sparrer don't run into that big bloke with the red beard.'

* * *

In the thick fog, Wiggins led the little band to Merriman's.

'Why didn't Sparrer come along?' Shiner asked Beaver, as they walked shivering along the dimly lit alleys.

'Dunno,' said Beaver. 'Sparrer's an odd kind of cove at times — he has his secrets, does Sparrer.'

Queenie agreed. 'He looked crafty, did little Sparrer,' she said. 'He's got something up his sleeve.'

Shiner thought about it for a while. 'Sparrer was staring at that handkerchief the old girl dropped,' he said. 'What do you think, Wiggins?'

'I dunno about Sparrer,' said Wiggins as they reached Merriman's shop and peered through the window, 'but I know there's been some dirty work going on here — see!'

And he pushed on the door, which had obviously been jemmied, for splinters and the wreckage of a lock littered the doorway. Great force had been used, and for a moment Wiggins held back.

Then he pushed forward.

'Mr. Merriman?' he called. 'You all right, are you?' He went ahead cautiously, trying to see into the gloom.

The others crowded behind him, pushing him forward but unwilling to slip past him. Then there was a creaking, groaning sound from inside the shop, and Wiggins could make out a weird, swaying figure.

'What's that?' shrieked Queenie.

Wiggins flinched, but a hollow voice came from the darkness. ' — came back!' the voice cried, and it was Merriman. 'I saw the same — but not the same!'

And with those barely audible and

totally mystifying words, the tobacconist crashed to the ground and was silent.

'It's Merriman!' yelled Wiggins, striking a match.

'Here — see, the place has been done over!'

'How's Mr. Merriman?' asked Beaver.

Queenie screamed as she saw the pale face and the blank stare.

'He's a goner,' said Wiggins. 'Poor old Merriman — see, he didn't get a chance to blow his whistle,' he went on, disentangling the silver whistle from the tobacconist's fingers. 'Go on,' he told Beaver. 'The Law has to be brought into this.'

He lit an undamaged oil lamp and looked around the shop, whilst Queenie and Beaver summoned help. Drawers had been pulled from cupboards and hurled about in a frenzy, tables were overturned, and bowls and jugs smashed open; Wiggins, however, had been at the scene of a number of burglaries, and he saw something wrong about this one.

'They wasn't after his takings,' he said.

He pointed to the shine of gold and

silver in the cash drawer.

'Then what was they after?' demanded Beaver, who had returned after energetically blowing Merriman's police whistle.

'P'raps he knew!' whispered Queenie, indicating the corpse. 'What was that he said just before he pegged out? Something about how it was the same and not the same, wasn't it?'

'And about someone coming back,' agreed Wiggins.

'Mr. Holmes would puzzle it out if he was here,' said Beaver. 'He'd smoke his pipe, then he'd have a think, and he'd have it all worked out.'

'So he would,' admitted Wiggins. 'An' that's what I ain't been doing!' he exclaimed, startling the others.

'What — smoking?' said Queenie.

'I ain't been thinking!' said Wiggins. 'I ain't been thinking about what they was after, that's what! Queenie you and Shiner stay here to see the Law. Beaver, you're coming with me.'

'Why?' yelled Queenie. 'I don't want to stay with a body!'

'You do as you're told, girl,' said

Wiggins firmly. 'Beaver and me are going after Sparrer, and if I'm right there's going to be more rough work tonight. No, Queenie, you talk to the Law when they get here.'

'What if it's Inspector Lestrade?' said Queenie. 'How can I tell an Inspector of Constables as you've gone out when there's a murder been done here, Arnold Wiggins?'

Wiggins could hear the clash of heavy boots on the pavement, and he knew he hadn't much time.

'Tell him Wiggins has a clue, that's what! Come on, Beaver!'

'But where are we going?' puffed Beaver, as they ran into the darkness.

'After Sparrer,' said Wiggins.

'But where's Sparrer gone?' Beaver gasped.

'Into more trouble than he can handle!' said Wiggins, increasing his pace.

4

'Wiggins ain't the only one who knows Mr. Holmes's methods,' Sparrow assured himself as he reached the side door of the Alhambra music hall. 'I was the one what found the clue, so I'm the one what's going to follow it up,' he went on, forgetting Rosie's part in obtaining the white silk handkerchief with the odd pocket.

'What do you want?' demanded the doorman as Sparrow entered the side-door. 'This door's for artistes and such — hop it, you.'

'I'm Sparrer.' 'Don't you remember me, Bert?'

Bert the doorman looked closer and saw that beneath the swathings of ragged scarf and the over-large cap was an old friend.

'Yeh,' he said. 'What do you want, then?' '

'You know about magic things, don't you, Bert? See 'ere — what's this, then?' said Sparrow, passing Bert the blood-stained handkerchief.

'Had a nosebleed, Sparrer?' asked Bert, examining the square of silk.

'Nah — accident. How about it, Bert? That pocket thing in it — recognise it?'

'Easy,' said Bert. He demonstrated for Sparrow. 'I've seen it done a hundred times on stage. The illusionist holds the egg or whatever in his hand. Over goes the trick handkerchief, a wave of the other hand to distract them, and away goes the egg. He calls it magic, but it's the oldest trick in the book.'

'Who does?' said Sparrow.

'Who does what?' said Bert.

'Who calls it magic?' Sparrow persisted.

Bert sighed. 'Didn't you see who's on at the hall this week? Orlov! The Great Orlov he calls himself. And he's not bad either, isn't Orlov, even if he does use the oldest trick in the book with this here handkerchief. See — it's got his initial on — 'O' for Orlov.'

Sparrow was staggered. He had followed up a clue, but here was more than he had expected, far more. He had expected the doorman to give him some ideas about who might have used the handkerchief, and here was Bert telling him that its owner was now appearing at this very music hall!

'Wiggins'll be sick!' he couldn't help saying.

'How's that?' said Bert.

'Nothing, Bert!' Sparrow told him. 'Is this bloke — the Great Orlov — still here?'

Bert shook his head. 'Finished and gone. Tonight was his last appearance. D'you want me to hang on to his hankie in case he comes back?'

'Nah,' said Sparrow, his heart beating faster. 'Tell me where he lives and I'll take it to him — maybe it's worth a tanner to him, it being part of his act.' Bert laughed and gave Sparrow an address a few streets away.

'There's no flies on you, me old cock-sparrer!' he called as Sparrow ran out into the thick swirling fog. 'I hope he does get his tanner, but I don't fancy his chances. Orlov ain't full of the milk of human kindness, but then he's a foreigner, ain't he?'

Sparrow pelted through alleyways and

down narrow, cobbled streets and dodged the occasional cab that splattered mud over him. And all the time he found himself getting nearer to a particular alleyway which he knew.

'I've been here before!' said Sparrow, peering into the ill-lit alleyway at the rear of the street where Orlov lived.

Sparrow's heart pounded as he approached the end house.

'That's the one Bert said he lives at,' thought Sparrow. 'And round the back is where that red-bearded bloke vanished — it's like Rosie said, it's all magic, only nastier. I wonder if Orlov's in?'

He peered through the windows at the front of the small, terraced house, but though there was a candle guttering in the parlour he could see no sign of the illusionist.

'I'll go round the back,' Sparrow decided.

Quietly and stealthily, Sparrow slid down the alleyway until he located the yard door of the end house. It was open. Sparrow hesitated. Should he investigate, or should he report to Wiggins and the others?

Sparrow peered inside. There was a

patch of light from the back door of the house — the back door was open too. He shivered with more than the cold of the swirling fog. 'Nah,' he thought. 'I'll go back for — what's that?'

Heavy footsteps rang on the cobbles of the alley

Someone was coming!

Sparrow almost passed out with terror. He felt his heart fluttering madly and he was sure that the big figure that loomed nearer and nearer could hear it. Without another thought, Sparrow darted through the yard and into the house — there was no time to look for a hiding place. He was into the house as the metal-tipped boots rang in the backyard.

'Where?' groaned Sparrow as he surveyed the bleak little room.

On a battered table were gleaming tools and bundles of brownish-looking candles, together with a number of iron canisters; three chairs and a chest made up the rest of the furniture. And, from another part of the house — from somewhere at the front — Sparrow heard a thick foreign voice calling.

'Bukovsky?' it called, then there was a gabble of some weird language that sounded as if the speaker had his mouth full of cabbage.

'In there,' Sparrow told himself, moving swiftly.

It was a built-in cupboard, large enough for Sparrow and not much more. Sparrow had it open in a second, and then he was wriggling into an assortment of illusionist's equipment and old clothes, certain that he must be found and murdered within seconds.

In his last glimpses of the back room, however, he had noticed a number of things. One was a large revolver on one of the chairs, together with a box of ammunition. Another was that the cupboard which sheltered him contained some familiar items, including a red beard and a ladies' winter outfit: and there was one more thing that in itself convinced Sparrow of the danger he was in.

It was a shiny black leather despatch case, and on it was the golden insignia of a Crown.

'It was him!' Sparrow whispered. 'The

old girl — it was him!' Everything began to fall into place, although it was several minutes before Sparrow was calm enough to work it out.

Even then, he found himself listening to a long, monotonous conversation in a language he didn't understand; all the time, sweating with terror and with the red beard finding its way under his collar as he burrowed into the Great Orlov's equipment!

Sparrow wished ten thousand times that he had not been so adventurous. He told himself that he had been stupid to be jealous of Wiggins and go off on his own. He promised himself faithfully that if he didn't sneeze and alert the big man he would never, never try to be a detective again.

But after a while, even terror became boring and Sparrow listened more carefully to what the two men were saying. Their conversation seemed to last for hours — days.

Every so often, Sparrow heard a name or a phrase repeated, so he was able to work out the men's names. Orlov wasn't

Orlov, he was Orlovitch. And the big bloke was Bukovsky.

Then Sparrow grew more alert.

'What?' he thought, as a familiar-sounding name which a foreign accent couldn't entirely conceal was repeated. 'He said Sir Alfred Connyngham!'

And then, amazingly, the two men began to converse in English!

'In one week,' said Orlovitch. 'And when he dies, we will make the Revolution!'

'When who dies?' wondered Sparrow, concentrating harder now. 'Are they going to do Sir Alfred again?'

Sparrow stored every word as gradually the men went over the details of their plan. The trouble was, however, that he was becoming sleepy.

Whether it was the lack of air in the cupboard combined with the build-up of body heat, or whether Sparrow was just plain tired after being out in the bitter cold since dawn that day, the fact was that he fell asleep.

He heard a great deal, but he was fortunate enough to miss the worst threat to his continued existence.

'And the props from your act?' said Bukovsky, who was packing away the tools and apparatus on the table. 'The despatch case and the clothes — what of them?'

Orlov shook his head.

'Leave them. From tonight, Orlov is finished. Dropping the handkerchief marked me as Orlov, and the trail must lead to here. A few more clues of the same kind won't harm us — we leave here now for good. Come!'

Bukovsky blew out the candles. Then his sharp hearing almost led to the finding of the sleeping boy. 'You hear something?' he said to Orlovitch.

Orlovitch listened. 'Nothing.'

'Something like — like a cat purring?' persisted Bukovsky. Orlovitch shook his head impatiently.

'We've waited long enough — delay is dangerous. Come!'

All of this passed Sparrow by as he dozed for another hour or so — the time it took Wiggins and Beaver to find him. Sparrow snored gently, and the streets around him grew quieter until there was absolute silence in the dark old house.

Sparrow heard Beaver's voice first.

'Ouch!' he cried as he crashed into a fallen chair, for the house was in darkness.

'Shut up!' whispered Wiggins.

'Why? There ain't no one here,' said Beaver.

'You hope!' said Wiggins, striking a match. 'No, they've scarpered.'

'And how about poor old Sparrer?' whispered Beaver, as he thought of what might have happened to his friend.

'Yeh,' agreed Wiggins, lighting a pair of candles. 'What's that?' he gasped, as he heard a faint, regular sound.

'What?' yelled Beaver, jumping away from him.

'I can hear something — low and horrible!'

'Orlov!' whispered Beaver. ''Orrible Orlov!'

'It's coming from in there,' whispered Wiggins.

'Let's get out of here!' yelled Beaver.

'Let me out first!' yelled back Sparrow.

'Yowwww!' roared Wiggins and Beaver, heading for the back door.

'It's me!' yelled Sparrow. 'Me — Sparrer!'

'Where?' cried Beaver.

'Where do you think!' yelled back Sparrow. 'In the blinking cupboard!'

It took only a moment or two to disentangle Sparrow from Orlov's stage props and Bukovsky's beard, and not many minutes for Sparrow to tell his tale — and an alarming story it was.

It raised as many questions as it answered, but at least one part of the mystery was explained.

Wiggins examined the female clothes, then the shopping bag, and the red beard, and, finally, Sir Alfred Connyngham's despatch case.

'It was all a trick,' he said. 'Illusions, as you would say.'

'Course it was!' said Sparrow. 'That's what the Great Orlov does for a living, ain't it? He dressed up as an old girl, then his pal Bukovsky comes along with his red beard and his cosh to make it look as if he's knocking her about.'

'But he ain't,' said Beaver.

Wiggins agreed. 'Then when Bukovsky runs off, the old girl gets taken into Merriman's — but she's Orlovitch, so when he's alone he gets his own clothes out of the shopping bag, does a quick change, then he hops it outside.'

'Wiv the despatch case in the carpet-bag he had all the time folded up,' finished Sparrow.

'And now it's empty,' said Beaver.

'Course it is,' said Sparrow. 'They was after the papers inside it, wasn't they? And now they've got them, and there's going to be all kinds of trouble!'

Wiggins and Beaver listened to what Sparrow could remember of all he had heard. It was a story of violence and outrage, bloodshed and revolution, anarchy and war.

'And it starts,' said Sparrow, 'when they blows up this Archduke. That's what Orlovitch said when he wasn't speaking in that heathen language. 'Bukovsky,' he tells this big bloke, 'we will dynamite the Archduke in just one week'!'

'Dynamite him!' breathed Beaver.

'Yes,' said Sparrow. 'Somewhere near a chimney or something, but I didn't gather much about that, it was all in heathen.'

'And what else did you hear?' demanded

Wiggins. 'Before you fell asleep, Sparrer.'

'You'd have been stifled in there too, Wiggins!' exclaimed Sparrow. 'Didn't I listen till I was nearly choked — and wiv a red beard tickling me neck all the time? What if I'd have sneezed? That big ugly bloke would've murdered me, he would!'

Wiggins soothed the angry little Cockney and got the rest of his incredible story. Sparrow had been drowsy for much of the time, and Orlovitch and Bukovsky had only occasionally spoken in English. But Sparrow had heard over and over again the same phrases.

''Three tons', so Orlovitch said,' Sparrow recalled. 'Him and Bukovsky said it maybe half-a-dozen times. And they're going to do him today week.'

'Next Monday,' said Beaver. 'Cor!'

'Near a chimney?' said Wiggins.

'Yeh,' said Sparrow. 'Wiv three tons of dynamite. Then he said, clear as you like in English, 'They'll not be looking for us, disguised as we will be, Bukovsky — Long Live the Revolution!''

In turn, Wiggins described how he had used Mr. Holmes's methods to find

Sparrow, and they were all about to congratulate themselves on solving the case of the Missing Despatch Case when they heard loud sounds from the front and back of the house.

'It's that big bloke what done Merriman in!' gasped Beaver.

'What coshed Sir Alfred!' groaned Sparrow.

'What Orlovitch pals up with!' cried Wiggins.

Then Wiggins recognised a loud, authoritative voice ordering men to have their revolvers ready.

'Lestrade!' said Wiggins. 'The Law's here!'

'Just when we found who really stole the despatch case,' said Sparrow.

'And why,' added Beaver.

'You in there!' bellowed a stern voice. 'Hands on your heads and come out quiet-like, if you understand English. And if you don't, look at this, what'll blow you to Kingdom Come if you resists arrest!'

The snout of a large pistol was thrust through the door.

'Why, it's a gang of street urchins!'

bellowed a constable. 'Sir, I think it's those ragamuffins again!'

Inspector Lestrade poked his nose into the room above another large pistol. He sighed.

'I thought they'd be here,' he said. 'Why am I plagued by amateurs when I'm in the middle of the most important case of my whole career? See to them, Sergeant,' he told me (for I was still on duty that evening). 'And then get rid of them!'

5

I pointed out to Inspector Lestrade that he was being unfair to Sparrow, but the Inspector became quite irate when I attempted to argue with him.

The way he saw it was that Rosie was in the wrong for tampering with evidence in the first place. Inspector Lestrade held that she shouldn't have kept the handkerchief once Orlovitch — in his disguise as an old woman — had dropped it. It was my view, though, that but for Sparrow's quick-wittedness, the trail leading to Orlovitch and Bukovsky would have been impossible to follow.

'Nonsense!' Inspector Lestrade declared to me, when the Baker Street Irregulars had been sent off with a flea in their (not very clean) ears. 'Routine police methods would have brought about the same results, but quicker! Now, don't let me hear anymore about those wretched ragamuffins and their escapades!

'I have informed my superiors that I expect to arrest these revolutionaries before long, and I have Sir Alfred's complete confidence. As for this nonsense about three tons of dynamite — whoever heard of such rubbish? Why, three tons of dynamite would be enough to blow up half of Central London, and to my certain knowledge these anarchists use only small bombs for their villainies!'

And so, as far as Inspector Lestrade was concerned, that was that.

He dismissed all that Sparrow had heard as so much nonsense — the product of his dreams while he slept in Orlovitch's cupboard. The important thing, so far as the Inspector saw it, was to guard the Archduke who was the central figure in the plot.

There was no secrecy about the coming visit to this country of Archduke Alexander of Rosnia. All the newspapers had reported that he was paying a ceremonial visit to Her Majesty; of course the real purpose of his visit had not been disclosed. Orlovitch and Bukovsky were now in possession of the secret reasons behind the Archduke's stay at Windsor with Her Majesty, and they were determined to prevent him from fulfilling them.

'The Archduke's the target of these anarchists,' Inspector Lestrade told me. 'Where he goes, I go — that's the way to do police work, Hopkins. Safety first!'

'And Orlovitch and Bukovsky, sir?' I said to Inspector Lestrade.

'Every officer in the force is on the look-out for them!' said the Inspector. 'Photographs of the anarchists will be displayed at every station in London by this time tomorrow. I'll have them in twenty-four hours!'

Wiggins thought otherwise. When he saw the late newspapers the following day, he said:

'Don't they know they're lookin' for a couple of expert illusionists? Does Lestrade think they're going to walk past his bobbies with a revolver in one hand and a smoking bomb in the other with a label on their hats sayin' 'Anarchists'?'

Beaver, who had provided the late edition of the morning's news, gazed at the breathless account of the night's adventures:

'VICIOUS ASSAULT ON PEER
OF THE REALM!
TOBACCONIST SLAIN IN
ANARCHIST PLOT!
INSPECTOR LESTRADE SPEAKS OF
IMMINENT ARREST!'

Together the rest of the Baker Street Boys read how the police had been summoned to the scene of the attack on Sir Alfred Connyngham, and then how Inspector Lestrade and his detectives had linked that outrage with the murderous attack on Merriman.

' 'Strewth!' whistled Wiggins when he had finished. 'Not a word about the Archduke. Lestrade's pursuing his enquiries amongst the theatrical fraternity, so it says here, but it don't say it was Sparrer that found the Great Orlov. And not a word about any missing documents either.'

Nor was there any mention of a plot against the life of Archduke Alexander in the newspapers during the next few days.

Wiggins and the others impatiently read every account of Lestrade's progress — though that wasn't much — and every day their annoyance grew.

'He still says an arrest is imminent,' said Wiggins.

'What's imminent? When he can't think of anything else to say to the reporters.'

His gaze came to rest as it often did on the stern features of Sherlock Holmes.

'I wonder what he'd do?' he muttered.

Queenie was quite sure about it. 'Well, for a start he wouldn't let Lestrade warn him off, not when he'd got a bunch of clues like what we've got.'

'We ain't got no clues,' said Shiner. 'Only what Sparrer heard.'

'And what's those but clues!' blazed Sparrow. 'We know when they're going to blow up the Archduke — next Monday. And I did hear them gabble on about three tons of something and about chimneys!'

Wiggins was thoughtful.

'See how Lestrade looks at it,' he told them. 'He thinks Sparrer's barmy — didn't he ask if we thought the Archduke was going to stand on a chimney while Bukovsky and Orlovitch stood around at the bottom ready to blow him sky-high with three tons of dynamite?'

'So he did,' agreed Beaver. 'And it is barmy!'

Reluctantly, they agreed that they had nothing to go on. It seemed that for them anyway the case of the Missing Despatch Case was over, but the next day brought a summons that was to change matters completely. It came in the form of a note from Dr. Watson.

'I have important news for you,' the note read. 'Bring the rest of the Irregulars and make sure they wipe their feet on the mat, or Mrs. Hudson will be displeased. J. H. Watson, M.D.'

'Dr. Watson wants us?' said Queenie. 'All of us?'

'With clean boots,' said Wiggins. 'Or his housekeeper will be mad.'

'What does he want?' demanded Rosie.

Wiggins spent another moment or two gazing at the picture of Sherlock Holmes.

'I got just about half an idea,' he said, but he would say no more.

Mrs. Hudson supervised the entry of the Irregulars with a careful and hostile eye, but they gave her no cause for offence.

'Ah — come into the study!' declared Dr. Watson. 'It will be quite suitable in the circumstances.' The children gazed about them in awe as they looked around the most famous collection of criminal relics in the world. They saw Mr. Sherlock Holmes's pipes, his microscope with a slide ready to be examined in it, his fencing-foils, his pistols on the mantel-piece and even his slippers.

'Phew!' muttered Wiggins, who was almost overcome with awe, but not quite.

'I'll be brief,' said Dr. Watson. 'I have here a telegram from Mr. Sherlock Holmes — '

'From Mr. Holmes!' cried Wiggins. 'But he's on his deathbed, sir!'

'Poor Mr. Holmes!' wept Rosie. 'He's a goner, ain't he?'

'Now, now!' cried Dr. Watson. 'No tears, if you please. They're quite unnecessary. I'm delighted to say that Mr. Holmes is making a steady recovery — '

'Smashing!' yelled Wiggins.

'Hurray!' yelled Shiner, with the others joining in delightedly.

Dr. Watson smiled at their enthusiasm, but his face became stern once more.

'Really, that's quite enough interruptions,' he told the Baker Street Boys. 'Mr. Holmes is still a very sick man, but when I heard lately that there was some improvement in his condition, I took it upon myself to inform him of the difficulties in the case you became involved in. And this is his reply. Listen.'

And Dr. Watson read out the message from Mr. Sherlock Holmes to the children:

''In the matter of the disappearance of Sir Alfred Connyngham's despatch case kindly inform the Baker Street Irregulars that their instincts are right. Lestrade has not the imagination to follow up their valuable clues, so they must busy themselves in the matter. Be sure to remind them above all that in this case things are not always what they seem'.'

Dr. Watson folded the telegram and put it in his pocket.

'I said it, didn't I?' said Sparrow. 'It's

all magic and faking, that's what.'

'As Mr. Holmes points out,' agreed Dr. Watson.

'So we're back on the case,' announced Wiggins, once more gazing around the room at the Master's possessions.

'And so you should be,' said Dr. Watson. 'Lestrade and young Sergeant Hopkins have been to see me more than once in the past few days, and it became clear to me that they were at a dead end. I took the liberty of informing Mr. Holmes of this case, and you have heard his reply. I can tell you that Inspector Lestrade is very worried at his lack of progress, and that meanwhile he travels everywhere with the Archduke to ensure his safety.'

'He's got no hope, with Orlovitch and Bukovsky around,' said Wiggins. 'Those two are too crafty for Inspector Lestrade.'

'No doubt,' said Dr. Watson. 'But where will you start, Wiggins?'

'Number 41 Park Lane, sir.'

'Where did you say? Ah, of course! At Sir Alfred Connyngham's residence.'

'That's right, sir,' said Wiggins. 'We

read as how Sir Alfred's recovering at his London residence, and maybe he's well enough to listen to a bit of sense now. Tomorrow's Monday, and that's when this Archduke bloke's due to be murdered. We ain't got no time to waste.'

'My sentiments exactly!' cried Dr. Watson. 'It could be Mr. Holmes himself speaking!'

The Baker Street Boys were in a cheerful mood as they reached the railings in front of Sir Alfred's Park Lane home, but their optimism was soon dampened.

It was a murky evening once more, with a heavy fall of rain and sleet, and what they heard on their arrival made matters worse. 'Here!' called a loud, authoritative voice. 'You lot — get away from those gates — scarper, fast!'

A large police constable in a glistening cape loomed out of the darkness to confront Wiggins and the others. Another equally large policeman patrolled the grounds inside the railings.

'Who's there?' called the second policeman. 'Pack of kids!'

'What they after?'

'We've got to see Sir Alfred Connyngham!' called Wiggins.

'Who?' cried the first policeman.

'It's true!' Queenie yelled. 'It's a matter of life and death!'

'They're going to blow up the Archduke,' said Rosie. 'And we know Sir Alfred — he bought some flowers from me the night he was attacked!' The second policeman now examined the urchins.

'What an 'orrible lot!' he said. 'Get off — scarper!'

'But we helped wiv the investigation!' cried Wiggins, stung by this unpleasant remark. 'We helped Inspector Lestrade after Sir Alfred got done by those two anarchists!'

'So you're those meddling busybody kids!' said the first policeman. 'I heard about you concealing evidence and getting in the way of the Law. And I'll tell you this: if you don't clear off in ten seconds, you'll find yourselves in a cell for the night!' Wiggins led the others away.

Only Sparrow could find an answer for the two burly police-constables. 'I hope that big foreign bloke comes round here!'

he yelled. 'Then you'll know who's telling the truth!'

A bellow of anger greeted this, and the Baker Street Boys took to their heels. Down one well-lit street they raced, and then Wiggins darted into a dark alleyway.

'Now what?' said Sparrow. 'We're finished, ain't we?'

'Who says?' demanded Wiggins. 'Here, Beaver and Queenie, you two come wiv me — wait here, you others.'

'Why?' they demanded.

''Cos you're too little to go where we're going.'

'Where's that?' said Queenie.

'Where the servants goes for a drink,' said Wiggins. 'I saw a public house — just round the back here — it's the nearest to Sir Alfred's, so that's where his staff'll be drinking when they drinks.'

'And then what?' demanded Beaver, as they came to a brightly lit and noisy public house called the Wheatsheaf.

'Dunno,' said Wiggins. 'But it's better'n being chased off by bobbies. Maybe we can get a message through to him, who knows?'

'And maybe we'll get a thick ear for being nosey,' said Queenie. Wiggins grinned.

'Do you think Mr. Holmes would let himself be scared off?'

Sparrow, Shiner, and Rosie were not left long in doubt, for Wiggins and the others were back within minutes.

'Wiggins done it!' cried Beaver. 'He's gone and worked out the clue!'

'What, where Orlovitch and Bukovsky are hiding?' said Shiner.

'Nah!' said Queenie. 'Where Sir Alfred's gone!'

'But he's round the corner in Park Lane,' said Sparrow. 'Ain't he?'

'No he ain't,' announced Wiggins. 'I saw one of the chambermaids; she'd had a few gins, and she let it slip before the under-butler could shut her up that Sir Alfred's gone to his country residence.'

'So what's the bobbies for if he ain't in Park Lane?' demanded Shiner.

'All bluff!' Wiggins said. 'The bobbies outside think he's inside, but he ain't — he's at The Chimneys.'

'At the what?' said Sparrow. 'Yeah!' he yelled suddenly. 'It's the name of a place

— they calls big houses fancy names. Of course — it weren't one chimney.'

'It was The Chimneys, near Newgate Village in Hertfordshire, more'n twenty miles on the train from here,' agreed Wiggins. 'And that's where we're going!'

They had reckoned, however, without the train timetables.

* * *

'First train out to Newgate?' they heard at Euston Station. 'You'll have a long wait. That's the milk-train leaving here at five-thirty a.m.'

Sparrow groaned in dismay, and Shiner tried to argue with the ticket-clerk, but all he got was a threat of a call to the railway police; and so it was Wiggins who had to take the lead once more.

'Home, all of you, excepting Sparrer,' he said. 'We'll wait for the first train and get out to see Sir Alfred.'

There was a howl of protest from the others until Wiggins pointed out that their total wealth came to one shilling and ten pence, which was exactly the cost of two single fares to Newgate Village Station. Wiggins went on:

'I'm going 'cos I say so, and Sparrer's coming with me 'cos — he knows the clues, that's why,' and this had to satisfy the rest of the Boys.

It was an uncomfortable night for the two of them, but they were hardy and thought nothing of it. An hour before dawn the steam-train clanked into Newgate Village Station, they got out and a sleepy porter gave them directions to The Chimneys.

'How long we been walking now?' said Sparrow, an hour later.

Dawn was breaking through low, hazy clouds but fortunately there was no rain or snow. Wiggins consulted his watch.

'Dunno,' he said. 'It's stopped again. We've gotta be near, though; we been walking for hours along these lanes.'

They tramped on and rounded a narrow bend at the top of a steep climb. An imposing wall began beside the road, and a little way down the hill was a set of iron gates decorated with a coat of arms.

Through the trees, Wiggins and Sparrow

saw their destination.

The Chimneys was an old, rambling mansion with Elizabethan timbers and red brick, but its most prominent feature was a remarkable number of high chimneys in its roofs. Getting over the gates presented no problems.

'I hope their dogs isn't savage,' said Wiggins, as he helped Sparrow down.

'And their servants isn't too handy with guns,' agreed Sparrow.

But they reached the huge porch without attracting any attention whatsoever. Before them was a pair of high wooden doors, again engraved with a coat of arms; and a bell-pull on a black iron chain.

'Here goes,' said Wiggins, pulling on the chain.

There was a deep, sombre clanging from the house. Dogs woke up on the instant. A deep baying sound left the two boys wishing they were back in London; and they felt their knees turn to jelly when a pair of servants opened the doors and confronted them with wide-mouthed shot-guns and the snarling teeth of half-a-dozen hounds.

'Who're you two young villains?' demanded a burly, older man.

'We ain't villains or any such things!' cried Wiggins. 'We got a warning for Sir Alfred Connyngham — '

'Don't you come with threats for Sir Alfred!' cried the second man. 'We got dogs for your kind!'

'But we got clues about the Archduke!' Sparrow called, seeing that they were being totally misunderstood. 'We came to help — we're the ones what looked after Sir Alfred when he got done on Monday last!'

'Was you?' said the second man, but the other one didn't want to hear anymore. 'Some ragamuffins did help his Lordship, that I know.'

'You two knows too much,' he decided. 'Lock 'em up, Yates, and send for the bobbies like Inspector Lestrade said we should if there was trouble — come on, you two, I've got a store-room with iron bars till the Law arrives! Sir Alfred ain't here, so we'll do what seems best.'

'But it's a matter of life and death!'

Wiggins tried to say. 'We know these anarchists is goin' to try to kill the Archduke!'

A growl from the older man was his only answer, but another voice came through the sullen snapping of the dogs and it was obviously someone who expected to be obeyed:

'What's this about the Archduke?' called a young man. 'Wait, Roberts — who are these boys?'

Roberts wasn't given a chance to explain. In a few short sentences, Wiggins was able to convince the young man — who wasn't much older than he himself — that he was acting in good faith.

'Best put them somewhere secure, sir!' cried Roberts.

'In my father's absence, I'll decide what's to be done!' cried the young man. 'And you, Roberts, can make a start by bringing some breakfast. These boys look famished, and if I'm any judge they've walked from the station this morning. Yates, clear those confounded hounds away!' He went on. 'Now, you two — I'm

Freddie Connyngham. Sir Alfred's not here, as you've gathered, and I want an explanation from you both. But first let me tell you I know about last Monday's attack. I'm grateful for what you did to help my father, but I realise that your business must be of the utmost urgency — so fire away, you have my entire attention!'

Wiggins and Sparrow took turns in describing what they knew. And then, over breakfast, Wiggins came to his conclusions.

'We know Orlovitch and Bukovsky are going to try to murder the Archduke,' he said. 'And we know that Sir Alfred's involved. But we can't square up the other things — not three tons of dynamite, unless it's to blow up this place.'

Freddie Connyngham whistled loudly.

'By Jove, I hope not! Now, let's get a few things straight,' he went on. 'The Archduke isn't here, nor, of course, is my father. They're due here though at about ten this morning, by special train, along with the Foreign Ministers of four more countries, and I can quite see that these anarchists would wish all of them blown sky-high. But I can assure you this place is too well-guarded for any desperadoes to enter — they wouldn't get past the dogs. As for three tons — '

He was interrupted by Roberts, bearing further supplies of food. 'The Three Tuns, did you say, sir?' said Roberts.

Freddie Connyngham dismissed the interruption.

'I wasn't talking to you, Roberts,' he said irritably, but Sparrow had suddenly sprung to his feet and hared off after the servant.

'Here!' the others heard him call to Roberts. 'You said 'The Three Tuns' — why'd you say that?'

'So he did,' said Freddie Connyngham slowly. 'And I can answer that myself!'

'It's a public house!' called Sparrow triumphantly.

'And it's near a bridge — '

'Over which the special train must pass to get on to our private siding!' Freddie Connyngham said, his face growing pale. 'Of course — you didn't hear the anarchists talking about a weight of explosives, you heard them naming a rendezvous!'

Wiggins shook his watch. Sparrow heard a clock chime.

'S'trewth!' he cried. 'We've got an hour, no more! And it took us a lot more'n that to get here!'

'The last clue,' said Wiggins. 'It all falls into place, like a pattern, as Mr. Holmes would say.'

'Arm yourselves, Roberts — Yates! Send the trap for help! Bring some of the men from the home farm — and fetch me a revolver at once!'

'Phew!' muttered Sparrow in admiration. 'Revolvers!'

'We're dealing with murderers!' said Wiggins. 'And they'd blow us up too if they could! Ain't we going in the trap?' he asked Freddie.

But the shortest way by far was not by road.

'We're going along our private railway line,' declared Freddie Connyngham. 'It won't take us more than half an hour with luck to get to The Three Tuns, but heaven help us if we're late, for the bridge there crosses a gorge a hundred feet deep, and no doubt the anarchists have mined it!'

Out of the house and into the woods went the boys and Freddie Connyngham, followed by Yates and Roberts and an assortment of delighted hounds. They ran along the track of the private line that linked The Chimneys with the public railway system. Before long, they had left the servants far behind.

'Keep going!' Wiggins called to Sparrow. 'Got a stitch!' he moaned.

'And me, old man,' groaned Freddie.

'Run it off!' growled Wiggins, lengthening his stride. 'How far now?' he asked Freddie.

'A mile — maybe a bit more!' panted Freddie Connyngham.

'We're cutting it fine,' said Wiggins. 'Come on!'

But Freddie Connyngham was no athlete, and Sparrow was near exhaustion after his sleepless night.

'I'll take the revolver,' decided Wiggins, grabbing the weapon from Freddie's nerveless hand. 'You two follow!'

'No need!' called Freddie, as Wiggins began to draw ahead. 'Look!' A small gang of railway workmen were eating their morning bread and cheese beside the track.

''Morning, sir!' they called, looking in puzzlement at Freddie Connyngham in the company of a pair of boys, one of whom was holding a large revolver. 'Need any help, sir?' said their ganger cautiously.

'That bogey!' cried Freddie. 'Can you get it on to the lines?'

'We could,' agreed the ganger. 'If that's your wish, sir!'

In a few moments, the three of them were bowling along the line at a high speed, and within five minutes or so Freddie hauled on the brake.

'We're coming to the regular passenger line,' he said. 'The Three Tuns is only a few hundred yards away — and there's the bridge! Here, let's push the bogey off the track and take a look.'

It was a wooden bridge, sturdy enough for occasional traffic, but without the massive strength of the iron railway bridges Wiggins and Sparrow knew in London.

Far below they could see a rushing stream strewn with jagged boulders. Wiggins gulped.

'Cor!' murmured Sparrow. 'If the train was to — '

'Exactly!' said Freddie, who had recovered his poise. 'But we're here and we can warn the driver to stop — come on!'

As the boys approached the bridge, however, Freddie paused. 'That's odd,' he said.

'What's odd?' said Sparrow.

'Those railwaymen — track inspectors by the look of them,' said Wiggins. 'Now why should there be two gangs out on the same length of track? Look, on the far side of the bridge. Only two of 'em,' he continued slowly. 'One a big bloke, an' one small and nasty. And both of them dressed like railway workers.'

'Yeh,' agreed Sparrow. 'It's them!'

'Who?' demanded Freddie Connyngham, as the two men on the far side of the bridge noticed that they had been spotted.

'The Great Orlov!' said Wiggins. 'And the bloke with the red beard! Watch out! They're shooting!'

Shots rang out, and the boys dived for cover.

'Then they have mined the bridge!' cried Freddie.

'And they'll pin us down till the train comes, and it's all up with father and the Archduke!'

'And a few foreign ministers and suchlike,' agreed Sparrow. 'And Inspector Lestrade,' he added thoughtfully.

Of course, it would have been the end of me too had the boys not acted, for I was on the special train with Inspector Lestrade. We were keeping a sharp look-out for anything suspicious, and the Inspector had even placed a couple of his men in the cab of the engine to watch the track. But all our precautions would have been in vain had not young Wiggins employed that combination of caution and daring which was so reminiscent of the Master.

'Here!' yelled Wiggins, as bullets whistled around his ears. 'Get the bogey back on the track — they can't hit us back there!'

It was true. The bogey was out of range of the revolvers, and it took only a little time for the boys to wrestle the heavy bogey back onto the track. Desperation lent them additional strength, but when it was in place both Sparrow and Freddie were baffled.

'Now what?' said Sparrow. 'I'm not going over that bridge on this thing, 'cos I'll get me head blown off.'

'It's a diabolical risk,' agreed Freddie, 'but I'm game!'

Wiggins was already providing the answer to their dilemma. 'Here!' he said, indicating a pile of railway sleepers, massive timbers stored as replacements for those that rotted. 'Get a dozen of these in front, then we'll be safe!'

And so it proved.

With only a minute or so to spare before the special train reached the mined bridge, the three boys had erected a barricade of heavy logs before them.

'Faster!' yelled Wiggins, as Sparrow and Freddie and he pumped with the last of their strength on the handles of the bogey. 'Come on!'

Bullets thudded into the heavy timbers.

'We're on the bridge!' panted Freddie. 'Not far now!'

'Then those anarchists can shoot us as we go by!' yelled Sparrow.

'Nah!' groaned Wiggins, whose own energies were practically used up. 'We'll jump just after the bridge and dodge into the woods — that's the best we can do!'

'But what about the train — it'll hit the bogey!' panted Sparrow.

'Better that than being blown sky-high!' said Freddie grimly. 'Well, Wiggins — well, Sparrow — good luck!'

Then they were all leaping from the bogey only yards short of where the gunmen lay.

As they jumped, Wiggins caught sight of an electrical battery and a pair of wires leading to the bridge. He also heard a roar of rage from Bukovsky. 'Well,' he said as he landed on a gravel incline. 'We did what we could — and I hope it's enough.'

It was. The three boys were too much concerned with their own immediate problems to take in what was happening, but I was very much aware of the events of the next half-minute.

A heavy shock ran along the train, hurling foreign ministers and senior policemen, to say nothing of important politicians, across their carriages.

The only casualty was the Archduke, who suffered a slight cut on his nose; he gained it whilst trimming his moustache in the bathroom of the special train.

He recovered sufficiently to join in the thanks and congratulations of Sir Alfred Connyngham, when he and the other dignitaries were told of their escape from death, and the part the boys had played in saving them.

'You have saved my life twice over,' said Sir Alfred beside the railway track, watched by a humbled Inspector Lestrade. 'I know everyone here joins me in this heartfelt expression of gratitude — we all owe our lives, and the peace of Europe itself, to you. I can tell you now that the Archduke Alexander is in this country to sign a treaty with the Foreign Ministers of four other nations, and because of your gallantry the signing will take place at The Chimneys. What do you say, Lestrade?' he said, turning to the Inspector.

And there, in front of the distinguished assembly, Wiggins and Sparrow listened to Inspector Lestrade's congratulations too. I later heard him say that regular police enquiries would have done just as well; but the truth is different.

There was some consolation for the Inspector, however.

Bukovsky and Orlovitch were later arrested in yet another of their disguises at Dover as they tried to board a steamer for the Continent. Wiggins had the last word:

'They didn't get away with it this time,' he said. 'Mind you, even Inspector Lestrade finally worked out that in the case of the Disappearing Despatch Case, things wasn't always what they seemed.'

Seeing Flynn

I knew I'd seen a ghost, for I knew what to look for: a dead person walking. And it had to be Flynn's ghost, hadn't it? See, he was staring at the three of them as they got to their knees, just like in chapel. He was there for as long as it took me to get my breath back, then he lurched off, the customary bottle of Jameson's in hand.

Only Gran was facing him, but she didn't wave or anything.

Later they agreed that indeed I had seen a ghost, so I got quite a reputation at school, which Mr. Jones quickly and sternly demolished. You can't have a seven-year-old seer at a Chapel school, can you? It's not proper. It could be dangerous.

I wasn't the danger, though, I realized gradually over the years.

She was. Gran.

'In this part of Wales, we are surrounded by seven kinds of religion, which assuredly means you that are not saved can take your pick of seven kinds of Hell,' said our old minister quite often and always too loud as if we were as deaf as him, so I knew all about dying and hauntings and noises in the night.

I peed my pants quite a few times going to school and back, for we had to go through the small cemetery to get there, and the older kids used to spring out from behind the mouldering gravestones, doing all the ghostly shrieks and moans, and once they'd come at us from behind a mound of earth beside an open pit. At seven years of age, I could urgently believe in ghosts, and I had no doubt that I saw one when Gran and Ma were in the garden with Auntie Flo, praying in our lilting language for Flynn's safe return.

Then I listened carefully and wondered if I'd got it right. The three women were praying to a moon that hid intermittently amongst blue-black clouds: but for what?

And what did I see there? It worried me till I bumped into my old school pal Harry Rowe in Brum when I was about twenty-nine. Had I seen Flynn's gangling, drunken corporeal and un-drowned self, the bottle of Jameson's in his big, red farm boy's hand, which we all knew too well when it was balled into a hairy red fist?

Or Flynn's ghost?

My Welsh faded gradually when I married a girl from Birmingham, both of us nineteen; she refusing to leave Brum, myself not unhappy to leave the sad little village, and especially my Gran.

Flynn's death? Well, he did pass away, but the way of it wasn't clear to me till after I had a chat with Harry.

I'll go back to that night when I saw, or didn't see, the ghost.

You see, I couldn't sleep that night. It was late-ish in the year, and there'd been a lot of excitement when I got back from Mr. Jones's class, this last period a history lesson about Glendower's feats against the brutal English, in the little parlour where we had a black and white telly — we were considered rich and posh by our neighbours, who called on us frequently to watch the football or *I Love Lucy*, which would always bring in half-a-dozen, but at the time I hadn't the least idea what made them laugh. Certainly, there was a good dozen of visitors to listen avidly to the promised extended bulletin repeating the *One O'clock News* statement to the effect that the ferry had gone down, taking all its crew and fifty-eight passengers with it — not a man, woman, child, dog or beast saved. All those lives gone under the waves, not ten miles from the safety of Holyhead!

Flynn had been on the ferry.

'So Flynn's gone from us,' said Gran. 'And about time, too.'

Flynn had got special leave from the RAF station. Off he'd gone — in civvies of course, since a British uniform wouldn't have been welcome in fiercely Republican County Cork — to claim his share of the loot from the sale of the family farm. Five sisters and one brother were squabbling for the pickings when the old widow woman died — smashing my ma's specs so she couldn't go out. She was extremely short-sighted and could afford only one pair. He'd stamped on them. So, no careful make-up, best silk stockings for her till she could get a new pair of specs, and it would take at least a week.

She'd be a faithful wife till he got back.

And I'd have some rest from his sadistic taunts.

'A boy in County Cork makes his own way in the world on his fourteenth birthday,' he told me the day after he moved in with us. 'I'll have your bag packed ready on that good day.'

It scared me more than the physical abuse. To be cut off from Ma — I wept for hours in bed every time he said it.

And now he was dead!

I saw his ghost because I couldn't sleep the night we'd learned of the loss of the ferry. It was the *Manx Castle*. But Flynn's watery end hadn't kept me awake. No, it was the sight of the wet black hair and the two clenched rows of white teeth and the yellowing shreds of burial clothes at the bottom pit the sexton had prepared for the eighty-one-year-old shepherd who had died a week before, and whose wife had pre-deceased him by forty-nine years, and whose shattered coffin we had been invited to view by the older kids, sworn to secrecy, of course. If Mr. Jones ever heard we'd hung around there for even more than a second, we'd have been thrashed.

Blodwen Hughes's skull and hands and burial gown haunted all of us throughout the day. After school, we congregated together.

'She hadn't got a nose,' said Fred Jones, a year older than me.

'Had,' said an older girl, whose name I forget. 'You lose all the skin and flesh and cartilage — '

'Cartilage?'

'Gristle, stupid,' she told me. 'Nice hair, she had.'

Her best friend, another name now lost to memory, though I can see her weasel-like face now, said, 'The coffin's thin, that's how Boozy broke into it. He must have gone too deep and stood on it. Fancy getting in with Blodwen!'

Boozy Brown was the sexton.

'Just right for one another,' said ghoulish Margaret Lewis, a girl I was in awe and fear of. She was pretty, tall and venomous. Mr. Jones always spoke softly to her.

'Boozy always stinks of beer, and Blodwen just stinks. Fine pair.'

'And they're planting her old man down there tomorrow. You're going, aren't you Davie?'

This was from a knowledgeable boy who wanted to be a fighter pilot, like those at the Yank base that Ma used tell Gran about before Flynn began to court her. Gareth? Yes. Gareth Edwards, a bit superior to us all. Posh.

I nodded. 'He's some kind of cousin to Gran.'

'Then we'll want a full report the day after,' he said.

'Every detail, mind,' Margaret ordered.

'Yeah, Davie!'

This was from my next-door neighbour but one's kid, my pal Harry Rowe.

'Shut up!' grunted the older kids.

'And stay that way,' hissed Margaret Lewis. 'Watch the coffin going down on Blodwen, then tell us what happened. OK?'

I told Ma and Gran at breakfast about Flynn's ghost.

Gran was in the middle of chiding me

about washing behind my ears; Ma said she'd ironed a white shirt for me and I was to wear my Sunday suit.

'And don't argue. It's only proper to show respect for the dead.'

'And Mister Hughes,' said Gran, 'is my second cousin once removed and there won't be anyone else but us at the funeral since they've all died off. So it's us. And Reverend Williams, naturally, but he doesn't count as a mourner. There'll be a couple of minutes of prayer, then we'll be off. I can't stand around in a cold wind for any longer. And you, you don't say anything, hear?'

'Yes, Gran.'

I'd hoped Ma'd say something kind, but her thoughts were elsewhere. She was fingering Flynn's black RAF uniform tie.

'Forget Flynn,' Gran said bitterly. 'He's dead and gone.'

I couldn't help myself. Christ, I was only seven years of age.

'I saw his ghost last night.'

The effect was most confusing to me. Gran grabbed my shoulder. Ma's face went white. The tie fell from her hands.

'You saw what?' said Gran.

'Flynn!'

'You couldn't!' Gran said.

My shoulder was beginning to ache. Ma reached out and gently detached her mother's hand. I did weep then, real tears, for Ma had intervened and rescued me.

My relief did not last long.

'I want to hear all about it, Davie,' she said.

'No, Ma, let him be. He'll tell us more if you'll not stare at him so. Here, Davie, wipe your tears on this.'

The tea towels were always clean. This one was thin and it scratched my skin.

'All right, Ma. I heard you and Gran and with Auntie Flo when you were out in the garden. Then you were on your knees, like at Sunday Chapel.'

'Not asleep? Why not?'

That had to remain firmly locked in my head. All children are natural born liars. The ability comes with the peer group. You have to learn to lie to defend yourself against adults, so you exchange strategies with your friends.

Margaret Lewis had been venomously

threatening earlier.

'I was thinking of poor Mister Hughes, Ma.'

Gran fixed her hooded black eyes on me.

'You hardly know Gwilym Hughes!'

'Ma!'

Gran heard the iron in her daughter's voice, so she swivelled her cold gaze away from me and began to rub her gnarled old red hands together. I watched them in fascination, for I could see my young scrawny neck in those old, strong hands, the way she took one of our chickens for the pot.

'So you couldn't sleep, Davie?' my Ma prompted. 'You're sensitive. I know that, as you should know. And you saw us, or you heard us praying, then you saw — a ghost?'

I nodded and the words tumbled out.

'He was in that long brown coat, and he had his hat on, and he had a bottle and that's what I saw, you know, the moonlight was on the bottle and when he put it up to his mouth I could see the white of the moon on the glass. Then he went, Ma. Oh, he did, Gran, don't look at me like that!'

'We were praying for his soul,' said Gran. 'Poor drowned soul.'

I was overwhelmed by the images, by Gran's fervent tone, but especially by Ma's tears. Why was she weeping for Frank Flynn, when he'd smashed her specs before he'd left to grab his share of the old woman's farm down in County Cork; and what would she say to her mates when she went to work at the telephone exchange?

'Oh, Ma!'

'I'm all right. So's your Gran. And if you say you saw a ghost, then you saw a ghost, Davie. You'd be half-asleep, and you'd likely had a nightmare, what with hearing about the *Manx Castle* and having all the neighbours in, all excited like. But don't say anything about a ghost to the Reverend, will you? We're going to Mr. Hughes's funeral soon, so up and wash all over again and be ready in a few minutes.'

'And do as your Ma says,' added Gran. 'You hear?'

I fled, got ready in under the minute and left the tiny bathroom for them.

I wanted to get out of the house, so I put my mac on and opened the front door softly and looked down the tiny front garden and put my hands out to welcome the cold rain. I heard a rumble of thunder coming from the mountains and welcomed the cheerful menace of the row. I've always enjoyed a good storm.

'Look at you all posh!' called my best mate Harry Rowe, also out at the front door. 'There'll be lightning, see, and you'll get your breeches burned off down the cemetery and your bum fried!'

That was how we spoke at seven. All kids do. Mine did, my grandkids do, I daresay, but not in front of me in deference to my years.

Harry had news. He shouted,

'There's a ghost in the graveyard, Davie!'

'Another one!'

I was between anxiety, wonder, terror and inquisitiveness, what with Gran so nasty at me and the growling from the mountains and my sighting of Flynn, so here was another strange thing! Harry hadn't heard me.

'Coming from the grave!' bawled

Harry. 'Gareth Edwards's Da was at the pub and at closing time him and Tom Kite and George Powys all started for the short cut though the graveyard, see, but they heard these noises like groans and moans and it weren't the thunder, so they say! So they went back to the road and they took the long way back to the village, and my Ma says it's all nonsense, and she was talking to Missus Jones just now, and — '

That was all, for he was yanked hard back out of the rain, so I had to laugh. But he'd badly frightened me. I'd seen Blodwen's grave, I'd see it again soon, and I dreadfully didn't want to go to the funeral of an old man I'd spoken to only twice, to the best of my recollection.

'You get in out of that rain!' snarled Gran. 'Now get to your room and wait till you're called and remember to act decently in Chapel, now, or Reverend Williams will send you to Hell!'

All I could think of was which of the seven Hells I'd go to.

The thunder rolled as we went through the graveyard, me huddling under Ma's umbrella, Gran striding out ahead. I studiously avoided looking at the open grave where Blodwen lay awaiting her husband for the past half-century. But I couldn't help sneaking a glance at the mound of red-brown earth that would soon cover her shattered coffin and her long, dark hair.

Reverend Williams gave us a long time on suffering, and not much on Mr. Hughes's good qualities, and we sang a lot of hymns. I studied a big God with a hairy face but a sort of twinkle about his eyes and a hint of a smile on his face. Then off we went with Boozy lending a hand as a pallbearer since one of them hadn't turned up.

Mr. Hughes's coffin preceded us, with the Reverend heading the slow procession through the driving rain to the graveside. There had to be a couple of minutes' wait for the slings to be put in place. My Ma took me by the hand. Gran was on my other side, but she didn't offer me her own gnarled hand, for which I was grateful; and then I looked down, fascinated, into the pit and I wish I hadn't, most fervently, to this day. For I saw a hand move, distinctly saw it move, to Blodwen's hair, now awash with muddy water, but still distinctly her hair, for it was as black as Rhondda coal. And I could see her teeth, and I wanted to scream, Look, Ma, there's Mrs. Hughes, dead fifty years and she's moving!

'Look, Ma, Oh, please look, Ma!' I whispered as the thunder rolled in the mountains, and a flash of lighting illuminated the school against the black sky, and I shuddered when I thought of Harry Rowe saying there'd been moans coming from the grave, and, please, please, look!

No specs! No help from Ma, then.

'Don't say another word, you!' hissed Gran, but I was babbling now, quite unable to stop.

'Reverend Williams, do you see it, down there?'

Thunder boomed loud and covered my yells.

The men were half-drunk, I guessed wildly, and our minister was deaf.

'But look down there! Everyone! Please!'

In the red-brown mud I could see a

shape, surely an outline of a shape, and where the coffin had been exposed this brown shape now covered it in part. The hand was still there on the rotted green of the face with the eyeball hanging loose, stroking the coal-black tendrils of Blodwen Hughes's hair —

And then I heard the low, distressed sound of a man in a terrible anguish.

I can still hear it, but not so often now. It comes to me maybe once, twice a year.

But it is as terrifying now as it was when I was a sensitive, repressed, bullied and beaten kid of seven. The pallbearers were ready.

'Ma — '

Gran dug her thick, gnarled fist into my thin ribs. The pain blotted out my senses. I staggered a little, but Ma steadied me. Then I would have lost my footing, for my foot slid on something hard and round, and I looked down quick and it was a bottle.

Gran looked, too. Our eyes met, and she had her fist at my ribs, just a warning this time. I said nothing. Looking back from a distance of four decades, I knew that she had me in thrall from that moment. I sobbed, and Ma heard.

'Now, don't get all upset, Davie,' she said, squeezing my hand tight; and I recovered just as Gran kicked two, three times at the wet soil.

It fell silently with the heavy rain onto Blodwen's teeth, and then the men were ready to lower the coffin and all was blotted out. Gran did take my hand then and let her nails sink into my palm. On my right, Ma peered myopically into the grave and held me for her comfort. On my left, Gran issued an ultimatum.

'If you say another word — '

Next to Ma, Boozy almost lost control of his side of the thick, wet belt.

His opposite number merely laughed.

'Get on with it!' snarled Gran.

Reverend Williams had had enough. 'We're all going to get our deaths!'

And then it was done: Mr. Hughes laid on his wife, ourselves told to throw a handful of soil down, and Boozy grabbing for his spade, for he wanted to be done quick and spend the fiver he'd earned for this extra pallbearing bit of work.

Ma was weeping.

Boozy's talented eyes saw the bottle. 'Jameson's? That's a good Irish whiskey.'

He turned it upside-down, then tossed it onto a heap of dead flowers beside his wheelbarrow.

The minister said the words, then we were off. There was no tea and whisky and ham and pork, for Gran had decreed that, since we were the total of the funeral party, we'd make our usual tea Mr. Hughes's funeral feast too.

'Now get changed and get to school,' said Gran.

'And you can take off Flynn's tie,' my Ma said tenderly. 'It's going back to the base with the rest of his uniforms.'

'Just wait,' said Gran, when I was out of the sodden best suit, and back in my tight-fitting school trousers and jumper.

'I've got to get to school, Gran. Mr. Jones said right away after the funeral.'

'I said wait! Tell me right now, *now*! About Flynn's ghost!'

'Gran, Ma said I'd been dreaming and there wasn't a ghost, and anyway I don't think I really believe in ghosts, and Mr.

Jones is going to belt me if — '

'In the blue uniform, wasn't he? All in that Royal Air Force blue, with that little blue forage cap, they call it, I know since he told me what they call it. He was in uniform, wasn't he?'

'No, he — '

'You saw that badge, all bright in the moonlight, didn't you, Davie?'

'No, it was the light of the moon when he was drinking from the bottle of — '

'Oh, no, boyo! Now tell me the truth, boy. You're my only grandson, Davie, dear. The ghost was Flynn, all smart and his cap badge shining bright in the moonlight, isn't that the right of it?'

She was wheedling me, telling me to agree with her. I had begun to put things together even before I'd met up with Harry Rowe by chance in a grubby little café near New Street Station where I worked as a porter. 'Flynn was in uniform, remember that. Always!'

'Yes, Gran. Can I go?'

'Good boy, Davie. There'll be currant bread for tea.'

After school, Margaret Lewis led the

inquisition. I wasn't a good storyteller, so I started with Blodwen trying to stroke her own hair, and for a moment they were stunned. Then they were going to belt me for lying, but Gareth Edwards said no, I was only a kid and what was wrong with a good lie?

I never did get to the empty Jameson's bottle.

I trudged over to the grave with Harry Rowe, but the wheelbarrow, dead flowers and the bottle were gone. It went from my mind for years.

'You still seeing ghosts, Davie, bach?' Harry grinned amiably.

'There never was a ghost,' I told him.

'No ghost, Davie? What about them moans and groans that night? That was a ghost, wasn't it?'

'Maybe it was thunder, Harry.'

It wasn't thunder.

'And that tale of yours about Blodwen's hair! Her trying to reach for it and all with her dead hand! You had us all peeing our pants!'

It wasn't Blodwen's hand, I wanted to tell him.

That was the moment of insight. Gran had done a good job of brainwashing me, but the memories were still there.

'Then there was you seeing Frank Flynn when he was as drowned as a dead rat in the Irish Sea, all ghostly in his blue uniform! Davie, man, that was another great tale!'

He had to have been in his uniform. Gran knew that. My memory of a flash of moonlight on an upraised bottle had to be expunged. Someone might recall Flynn's taste for Jameson's, and Boozy was garrulous in drink.

I could hear her saying it:

'Flynn's gone. And about time too.'

No one should die like that.

Flynn had not been on the *Manx Castle*.

Maybe he'd finished his business early and changed to an earlier crossing to get back to Ma. Not that speculation would help on such things, for I knew that Gareth Edwards' Da and the others had heard Flynn the night before the funeral, for Flynn was always slow to come out of his drunken coma, and he always complained and moaned for hours before he'd leave Ma's bed.

No doubt he'd taken the short cut to the pub after seeing the women praying. Had he heard them wishing him drowned? Maybe. Certainly, he'd veered off course and found Blodwen, not *The Bull*.

Had he thought he was caressing Ma's hair when we'd assembled to see Mr. Hughes put to rest? Was Flynn trying to kiss Blodwen's yellowing skull as the coffin took away the dim morning light and stopped the rain from falling on his sodden coat and Blodwen's grinning skull and Flynn's hand, all muddied where Gran had expertly shifted soil onto it?

The women praying in the garden so long ago were not praying for Flynn's safe return. No. They prayed that he would be on the *Manx Castle*.

'No ghost, Davie?'

I shook my head.

'Pity that.'

'Yes. Pity.'

Ma rang me not long after our chat in the café. She'd remarried and happily but now she sounded panicky. When she calmed a bit, she said that Auntie Flo said Gran couldn't sleep when there was a hint of moonlight in the sky. I could see the way things might be.

'Moonlight? That troubles her?'

It was Flynn's ghost that troubled Gran. No matter how tight she shut the curtains, he always came by moonlight, the RAF badge in his forage cap glittering stark white; and his muddied hands, just bones; and the red of the hair of his hands; and his arms open wide as he goes to Gran. He's calling her Blodwen, always Blodwen; and why should he call her that, now?

'As in Blodwen Hughes?'

' — and the eyeballs hanging down on his teeth, and the teeth all yellow, just like Blodwen Hughes's, that's what Gran screams it is, and the flesh of his face gone rotted green — '

'Like Blodwen's?'

'Isn't it terrible, just!'

It was feared she was losing her mind.

'What was that you said, Davie?'

'Pity.'

The Fly in the Ring

The old hag came out of the mist in black, head down, thin limbs scuttling, frail body bent. In a tenth of a second she was hurled momentarily forward, then slightly upwards, and then down, down, down, until her bones were snapping under Bernie Gayle's new Land Cruiser. The road was awash with the rain that had made him cut his speed on the home stretch from Grantham to a safe level, or what should have been safe for anybody, except that she had no road sense and was probably deaf. Had she marked the impeccable plum red of the paintwork or dented the bull bar or marked the fender, useless old cow? Had she? The nerve!

You couldn't take a four-by-four out without some careless sod wanting to contest your inalienable right to drive just as you liked: for weren't you forty-three, big and good-looking, no fat gut, with a solid business in the timber trade, and going home to a fine meal and a well-built new woman? — Who unfortunately couldn't quite handle the sour bitch of a daughter he was left with. And what was that he'd glimpsed momentarily after the impact? There, out in the field and the mist? What, a clump of tatty travellers' caravans and an open truck and a lumpy old Ford van? Yeah. So what?

Bernie checked the mirrors. Nothing.

Lucky again, yeah? Bernie does it again!

'Home free,' said Bernie, crunching gravel with the heavy tyres and admiring the shape of the 1990s stylish home he'd bought for his new woman, a placid creature appropriately named Daisy.

She wasn't at the door to greet him, naturally, for who'd choose to stand in a doorway with the rain still pelting down? Well, no one but a stroppy sixteen-year-old, going on seventy. Erika was looking for a fight. She'd heard the sound of the motor, and she wanted to give him a hard time. He didn't want to try placating her just right now, for to be honest, Bernie, he told himself, there's still a slight possibility that there could be gore somewhere under the motor, and you had to think about DNA these days. He especially wanted to have a good look at the heavy creature-killer at the front end.

'Be with you in a couple of minutes, love,' he called to his sullen daughter. 'You go inside and keep warm, Erika. Brought you something.'

'I don't want anything from you.'

'Something I have to do down the garden, Erika. You go in. I said a couple of minutes, but will you tell Daisy it'll be more like ten?'

She mouthed a foul word or two and stayed there, glaring at him.

'I couldn't pick you up, Erika! I'd got this Jarvis contract to see to — '

'You're useless!'

He'd made her look cheap in front of her mates when she'd been on the mobile but he couldn't just walk away from a hundred-grand contract, right?

'Be with you in a minute, Erika, love! Got something really nice for you, what with your GCSEs on the go and all! Why don't you go in, get changed out of that school clobber — got a job to do here, right? Make yourself gorgeous, do that thing!'

And still she stood, stone-faced, implacable, so Bernie struggled into the Barbour and fisherman's hat.

He'd thought it all out.

Take now, for instance.

He had to check the front of the motor, then maybe check the tyres for any bits of gyppo that might not have been scoured out by the swirling rain. Next? Well, not the underbody.

He couldn't very well go crawling underneath the motor now. In the morning he'd have a look, early. Better, of course, to leave the Land Cruiser on the gravel all night, so that there'd be no trace of anything incriminating on the floor of the garage. Let the wet drip all night, that was the right thing to do. And, no worries about a tinker hag. Who'd miss her?

She was watching him.

'You'll catch cold, Erika!'

'You don't care. You never have!'

Thunder rolling, the rain belting down, wouldn't you think she'd damned well get inside — ! Bernie could feel the anger rising. That was another thing about him that could be underestimated. The fury, the need to hurt. Bernie smiled at his daughter and got down from the cab.

Yeah, a quick look, then inside, yeah?

Erika was all ears and eyes and nose, he thought, somehow aware of trouble.

He could deal with her. Promise her something, get her in a good mood with a glass of Beaujolais and the fine little jewellers' box in the pocket of his mohair jacket, and — all right, can't see anything on the fender here on the driver's side, no scratches, nothing on the bull —

'Oh, Jesus Christ!'

He screamed and went down on his knees in panic and tried to look away from the — the *thing* clenched around the bright steel of the bull bar, with the fingers tight, and that arm broken off below the elbow —

'Aaaaaaarghhh!'

'What's wrong?' yelled Erika. 'I'm getting wet out here!'

Bernie was hardly aware of his daughter's angry complaint.

The old tinker bitch was in pieces and

one of those bloody pieces was on the bull bar of the Land Cruiser, but the worst of it was that the fingers were wrapped around the bright metal. How could they stay like —

Bernie howled again and then abruptly cut off his yell.

Terror had afflicted him, but he was Bernie Gayle and he could handle anything. He'd have to get rid of it fast, bloody fast. If that little bitch saw it, she'd be right off to the coppers on her mobile — she'd love to shop him, hated him for the way she said he'd treated Hilda, the thin argumentative cow. And Erika was ten times worse since she had brains as well, so let's get the motor under cover and do something about it!

Fast!

'What's the matter?' he heard, as he held out the remote for the garage. The garage door rumbled and would bloody well stay in place long enough for him to drive into it, since no way was he going to try to handle it, not without garden gloves.

It wasn't Erika calling now, it was Daisy.

So, answer calm, dear, well-upholstered Daisy — not much below her coiffure, but another potential witness. He called,

'Just wrenched my knee a bit, darling!'

'Oh, Bernie, love! Do you want a hand?'

Rage engulfed him.

He badly needed to kill Daisy.

She'd seen it, hadn't she? Just taunting him. I'll —

Now, Bernie. *Control*. How could she have seen it? No way.

'I can manage, sweetheart! Get back in out of the rain!'

Think.

'And get something nice on — and make sure Erika goes in a hot bath with a nice glass of something, the poor girl's soaked through!'

And keep out of my way.

Or else.

He drove the Land Cruiser into the wide, deep garage. Daisy didn't drive, so he had loads of space.

Bernie was shaking when he knelt to inspect the gyppo's remains, or such as were now clutching the bull bar.

It was then that he saw the ring.

His mood changed abruptly. 'Well, Granny Lee. What have you brought this lucky lad?'

It was an amber ring of a rare quality, the gold thick and chased around the setting of the softly glowing solidified ancient pine resin.

He slipped on a gardening glove, and gently pulled at the skinny wrist. The fingers wouldn't move.

'Come to Bernie, Granny.'

And it did. It was not rigid, not floppy. It weighed about as much as a hand rake — in fact it probably could be used as one, chuckled Bernie to himself as he placed the withered and chafed half-limb on the old office desk he used as a workbench.

It slipped off easily. He flicked on the lamp above the bench and examined it closely. Clearly the ring was old — that was, the band of gold itself, for of course the amber was old! How long had she worn it? Well, it was of no use to her now.

The fly in the ointment was that it was on the fourth finger of the left hand of the hag. Eight inches or so of arm still projected from the hand, though fortunately — for this was an appalling moment even for a man who prided himself on his lack of squeamishness — the ragged forearm's end was more or less sealed. No blood, no gore — rather a neat and surgical amputation, Bernie considered.

'Done it again,' Bernie told himself. 'Bloody done it again!'

Just then, he thought he saw a slight movement of the ring finger. It couldn't have been, no. Or was it something do with, what did his copper mates call it, *rigor mortis?* He patted the forearm affectionately.

'Have to do something about you. I'll see to you in the morning, Granny,' he promised, as he shut the desk drawer on it. 'And get rid of the ring.'

He went gladly into the awful weather.

'You should take your shoes off,' said Erika, in exactly his former wife's voice. 'You're treading muck all over the carpet.'

'Oh, didn't realize,' Bernie said diplomatically. It was not a time for a fight. And he wasn't too sure he wanted the casserole Daisy was putting on the table.

Well, maybe a few bites.

He could hear again the scratchings and thumpings of the thin old body as it disintegrated.

'So what happened at school today? Anything good?'

'You said you'd got something for me.'

Not 'for me, Dad', of course.

'Got it right here in my jacket pocket, love. Sort of present to buck you up for your GCSEs.'

'I won't pass any.'

But Erika took the locket out, tiny diamonds glittering brightly, her painted lips a bit open. Even she couldn't resist a gasp or two, could she?

'Oh, it's lovely!' said Daisy.

'Not bad,' said Erika.

'You going to put it on?' asked Bernie.

'Tomorrow, for school. Did you bring her anything?'

Her.

So Daisy was left out. But, seeing the hurt in those large brown eyes, and the thrust of her still firm and pointed breasts, he said,

'I might.'

And, unwittingly, unpremeditatedly and fortuitously, he had.

'What's that? Hey, it's a ring!'

'Daisy's prezzie, isn't it?'

'I thought she wasn't getting anything! It's my turn! Aren't I doing those damn exams all week?'

'Oh, it's lovely, Bernie!' Daisy mooed.

So it was a cheerful meal that evening, both women showing off their new bits of jewellery. Daisy wasn't inquisitive, but Erika was mildly interested in the ring's history.

'Did a bit of a deal at the pub, love.'

'It's got this fly in it, though,' said Daisy.

'It's supposed to have,' Erika told her. 'It's a rarity. I bet it's worth a lot. Some woman must have liked it a lot. See how it's so worn. I expect she'll miss it.'

Bernie secretly chuckled.

'Not now, love.'

At dawn, Bernie slipped out of bed, Daisy snoring, bless her. He hurried to the garage, flicked the light on —

'What's that doing open?'

The drawer had slid a little out of its

housing. It was open only an inch or two, but —

'I know where you're going, gyppo,' he said, but it was still gut-churning to put the half-limb in a stout garden sack, even with gardening gloves on.

He almost ran round the house to a patch of newly turned soil, realised he needed a spade, ran back, dug two feet down and left the old hag's skin and bones for the crawlies that must find it soon, the sooner the better. Then he moved a heavy pedestal in the form of a carp, with a platform on top for a matching terracotta pot, right now full of verbena and trailing lobelia. And — that was that.

Routine, lovely money-grubbing routine, took over, and Erika didn't bitch too much at dinner. So life was good again, or as good as it was going to be. Bernie checked next morning on the terracotta fish and the brilliant blue and red of the flowering plants. Incident, he told himself, closed.

Except that it wasn't, for when he got back from business, Daisy called,

'Bernie, we've got moles! Funny place

to have them, Bernie! I thought you'd got rid of them.'

She was standing beside the fish. It hadn't moved. But there was a pile of soil on the south side of the pedestal. Bernie's guts lurched and churned and filled with acid, just the way a hangover took you, not on the first recovery day, but the next.

Erika came out, bored maybe.

'It's more like a rat hole,' she told them, kicking the soil away and exposing a tunnel. 'Christ, look down there — behind the jasmine. It's a rat!'

Bernie blanched. It was too big for a rat, too long, too skinny and boney and withered.

'I'll put some poison down.'

That was what he did, but there was no long-tailed corpse around the garden, however much he searched when he got up at dawn the next day. He gave himself a moderately large glass of wine at about seven, just before the two women came down to have breakfast. And no, he told Erika, no lift today. Things to do.

When she'd gone whining to school, Daisy had a request for him.

'Drop me off at Jo Lai's, love? I've got an appointment for ten. Shall I get the highlights done again? And how about my nails?'

It's my eyesight.

That was it. Yes, Erika was right. It was a rat.

'I like that new phosphorescent Nile blue, don't you, Bernie?'

'What the bloody hell are you talking about?'

'Bernie! Don't talk like that to me! I love you, Bernie! We love each other!'

So he gave her a couple of hundred and drove back at a steady rate — think of the brandy, we don't want the law involved, no way — and pushed the pedestal over. He scrabbled in the soil, then went back for a hand rake and trowel, got on his knees and dug two, then three feet down, well beyond the newly turned soil, right down to a clay stratum.

* * *

At the salon, Jo said, 'I do love amber. It looks old. And that fly — it's perfect.

Some people wear amber as a symbol of trust, did you know? It's an old superstition. You don't look old. And you'll look radiant when we've done with you.'

The woman in the next chair looked hard at Daisy. Then she leant over.

'May I see the ring, dear?'

'I don't want to take it off. I never will. But do look.'

The woman was older than Daisy. She had thick dark hair, an ungenerous mouth and a dark complexion. Her eyes narrowed. Daisy didn't notice.

'It's beautiful,' she said. 'Someone must love you very much to give you that. Did you say your name was Daisy?'

'Yes! Daisy. I haven't seen you here before, have I?

'Can we start on your nails, Mrs. Gayle?' said Jo.

Daisy liked that about her. She charged the earth, but she was attentive and so, so respectful. She was a bit yellow. Could she be Chinese, or something?

The senior assistant wanted to get on with the dark-complexioned woman's hair. All she wanted was a shampoo, rinse and conditioning, she told the girl.

But she had something to say to Daisy first.

'The Delaneys always give their women a ring like that on marriage, Daisy, did you know?'

Daisy didn't know what a Delaney was, and she'd had enough of conversation. She didn't want to sound rude, so she asked about them.

'Travellers,' said the woman. 'I'm a Delaney. The ring goes to the grave with us.'

* * *

Bernie was at his office. It was on the first floor of what had been a fine brick-built residence just off the street. His secretary came in, smiled sweetly and wiggled encouragingly as she left. Bernie wasn't too interested, though he'd put her down as a possibility. He thought briefly of Daisy, very briefly.

'So that was the old hag, was it?' murmured Bernie, as he looked through the *Herald* to see who was building what and where, and who'd started taking out ads, especially in his line (wood). ''Mary Agnes Delaney' of no fixed address, aged seventy-seven years'.'

There were no witnesses, though the public was asked to give the police any information they might have. Bernie was not chuckling. He wasn't looking forward to returning home that evening. But he did go, as soon as he'd got Elspeth to check the e-mail and send out two bills and one signed contract.

'They liked the ring, Bernie, they all did! Jenny Stokes and I went to Mario's — lovely pizza, no chips of course, just a green salad; then some tutti-frutti, just a small portion. She loved it! So did Jo Lai, you know, the hairdresser — and that nice little manicurist, can't remember her name — oh, and that woman next to me — she said something about Delaney and rings like that — Bernie? Bernie, what's the matter?'

Bernie Gayle knew he was getting an ulcer. He knew about the Delaneys.

'Daisy, answer me something, and tell me the truth. Or it will be very rough for you. No, I don't mean that, stop your stupid bawling!'

He learned that this Delaney woman knew their names.

The phone call came in the middle of the game pie, sautéed potatoes, minted peas and broccoli with a cheese topping.

'Gayle?'

The voice wasn't harsh, not unpleasant, just a voice — not educated, not rough, just quietly commanding. The conversation was brief.

'We know, Gayle. You'll be seeing us. Not the law. Just us.'

Bernie just made the toilet beside the porch before he puked up his day's intake. The evening was long and the morning came agonisingly slowly.

The severed limb was on the dashboard.

Bernie screamed.

He couldn't drive the four-by-four, no way. So he panicked, slammed the door shut on the ghastly thing and saw a small can of paint thinners on the shelf above the desk. Gagging and gasping, he forced himself to look through the side window.

It had moved.

Now, it clutched the top of the steering wheel.

His cell phone rang and automatically he grabbed it from his jacket pocket.

'Gayle — Bernie Gayle. Today,' came the calm, utterly deadly, Delaney voice.

'No — ooooo!' he screamed.

Erika ignored him and walked smartly down the drive. Her half-heels crunched gravel. She didn't look back. Daisy had heard him.

'Bernie!'

She couldn't, mustn't see. No way could she be involved with the hand that now flexed itself and then — it bent — it bent — at the second joint — of the fourth — it couldn't — the fourth finger —

Bernie Gayle found something left of the man he had been three days earlier.

'It's nothing, Daisy, nothing at all. But if you'd like to go in the house and make me a decent coffee? Big pot of coffee? Hot? You're good at that.'

She rushed off almost happily, and Bernie collected all the inflammables in the garage. He made a pile of dried branches and an old rocking horse. Then he poured petrol over the lot from the reserve can for the mower.

'Burn the damned thing. Burn!'

He steeled himself to wear the gardening gloves once more. Eyes shut, he grabbed for it. Then he had to look.

It flexed that empty finger again. Bernie could see an indentation around the base of the fourth finger. He cursed and opened the door, grabbed hard, fought the amazingly tight grip, dumped the wizened, withered, arm and hand into a garden bag and ran.

The plastic sack rustled.

He put his foot down and felt movement. The match flared.

The flames came instantly.

'Die! Die, you Delaney bitch!'

He threw the sack, saw it flare and begin to melt.

Daisy slapped his shoulder and began to ask questions as he yelled obscenities. She had a tray, a silver coffee pot and small elegant cups. As he turned, his hand caught her shoulder. The silver coffee pot flew up and onto his face.

'Oh, Bernie, the ring's slipped off!'

He was blinded. The shocking pain bewildered him.

'Never mind the bloody ring!'

'Oh, Bernie, look — '

He couldn't. He wanted to put his fist into her face, kick her when she fell, boot her stupid head. He heard her scream.

'The rat! It's running! It's burning!'

'I can't see,' he moaned, and he couldn't, for the pain was in his eyes, wildly scalding his face and his hands. Daisy pushed and led him as he wailed and screamed, and in a few seconds she had his face pushed into cold water in the guest toilet through the porch. The cold water did its work, but he couldn't stop his mind from the coldness of fear, the chill of the grave, the freezing certainty that in life and in death the hag was at his heels.

Sheer, brutal determination caught up with him as his eyes cleared. It was a blurred small room he saw and a distraught and screaming woman he burst past as he made for the four-by-four.

All he could think of was escape.

From the black figure in the rain.

From the chill, hard voice of Delaney.

From — from everything.

He drove in a frenzy, not far — for he heard a scraping, scratching, fearful sound behind him, and he knew that Daisy hadn't seen a rat in flame. He wanted to get out of the motor, but he had his foot hard down. He got to the motorway junction and pushed the Land Cruiser's four litres so the motor soared.

He could not look back.

He felt his neck go cold. Then hot. Then it was probed by boney fingers.

The fingers advanced around his head, and he felt a thin, sharp nail probing his right eye. He screamed and tried to think of a way to avoid this dread. Wasn't he always lucky? Bernie who could get away with —

'No!!'

The finger slid around the eyeball and

gently insinuated itself into the softness of his brain.

The last thing he saw before the crash was the amber of the stone, and the shiny time-frozen blackness of the fly.

Dark Peak

'We're off to see the Bog Man,' we finished, as the train drew in. 'The Wonderful Bog Man of Gryse!'

There was no wonderment, though. And we did get to see what we had set out to see.

To our everlasting regret.

I was with, as they say, Melissa. Zara, our mutual friend, who was more or less settled in England now, had come along too, all of us thinking of careers and each other, and nothing at all about the what we might chance upon in the Dark Peak.

We'd come on a none-too-serious quest for enlightenment about the past.

We'd got lightweight hiking boots on, and we'd brought the advised emergency gear: an old-fashioned metal container with plasters and bandages and things, naturally a cell phone, enough food and drink, a torch, maps — all in an old rucksack I'd bought for next to nothing at a car boot sale. Myself and my lady were in shorts, me with my shirt looped round my waist, Melissa looking languorous and fit at the same time, tall and svelte.

She's black, startlingly so, against my white body, which is big and solid and won't tan. I just singe.

Zara's Persian, so she keeps out of the sun: an inherited trait.

She looked oriental and elegant and we all felt exhilarated as we looked up and down the one street of Grysethorpe for our starting-point, which was to see the old, very *very* old, gentleman himself.

We were all capable young people.

Melissa was going to be a teacher of infants one day, but her hobby was anthropology, hence the impulse for our trip. Zara had studied medicine in Teheran until the mullahs told her not to, hanging her father and brother to reinforce the point. She hadn't yet found a place in a medical school over here, but she had hopes that the Institute of Tropical Medicine might give her at least an interview.

We *were* off to see the Bog Man.

And where he'd been found amongst the Standing Stones, deep in the astonishing gruel of chemicals about two metres down in a peat bog, where he'd been murdered about three thousand years ago. But it had all been so wonderfully preserved, all of it, down to some shreds of vegetable and animal fibre that said he was wearing thonged sandals, leather breeches, and a wolfskin cloak. It could only be shown to an invited few, and we were invited.

Melissa had made the enquiries and got a no, but I'd fixed that. I had my Master's in Marine Biology, but it was the genetic research that had got us tickets to the very exclusive museum that was his last resting place — I have used a term that is not wholly accurate I realise: I have to pause. *It never rested*.

I'll spell the whole, terrible tragedy out.

Only a few shards of bone belonging to two of his attackers had been preserved, as I say; but the Bog Man, in a sense, had survived.

'I suppose we'll get postcards and such from the museum?' said Melissa. 'I hope they're scary. I want to send a few to my friends.'

'There's a happy thought,' I said. 'Right, Zara? You want some? For the Ayatollas?'

'I wouldn't do that, even to them.'

She's careful about her pronouncements. They have to exactly mirror her thoughts, otherwise she'd be unfaithful to her extremely demanding religion. They don't see shades of grey in thought or speech, the followers of Zoroaster.

Only black and white.

Good and Evil.

'He's just joking,' said Melissa. 'Anyway, my friends will go for this wolfskin cloak he was in. Cooky. Yes?'

'Oh, you, Melissa!' Zara said fondly. She looked content rather than happy. That is, until we asked for directions to the small museum where they kept the Bog Man, please.

There's usually a direction post to such institutions even in small towns, but not in the charming small town — village, really — of Grysethorpe.

'Where is it, my dears?' said the centre one of the three middle-aged women in

Barbour wellies, over-tight jeans and tank tops that didn't suit them, all with blondish streaked hair with a touch of grey, all very confident of themselves; this one with the cut-glass voice of the finishing schools.

Melissa explained the purpose of our quest.

'Oh, you've been *invited!*' said left flank, bright red tank top and a coral necklace.

'So pleased you've come to visit,' said right flank, flashing the big sapphire on her second finger.

The centre woman, making decisions, said, 'We'll take you there. And where are you three darlings from?'

Darlings.

All three of them were alert.

How could we know that these frightful hags would have such a devastating impact on our three young lives? But we sensed something, all of us.

Why should they wish to know anything at all about us?

Their gaze was concentrated, the three sets of eyes, on Zara. Did they sense her psychic and very special aura?

'From somewhere Middle Eastern?' suggested right flank silkily to Zara. 'Lovely textures. Beautiful patterns. And a short sari sort of thing, too. Ducky!'

Zara wouldn't answer.

'Oh, shy!' said left flank heartily. 'I like modesty in a young woman. And you, dear?'

'Fulham,' said Melissa.

'Really? It must be very interesting for you!'

'Ooo, isn't it just?' yowled Melissa lasciviously, quite able to deflect intrusive questions. 'Ooo, you should be there!'

The leader looked a question at me.

'Sheffield,' I said politely.

'Well, you're a big, big Steeler, aren't you?' said left flank, bulging over turquoise and fluorescent yellow. 'I suppose you play rugby rather violently?'

'Soccer. And cricket.'

'Oh, how simply ambidextrous of you!' right flank said.

'I like to boot things hard in winter. And hit them hard in summer.'

She smiled, and I found myself

wondering about her teeth. Was there a certain curl to the incisors when she laughed aloud at my discomfiture?

'Hit things hard!' repeated right flank, laughing aloud; not a pleasant laugh.

'Not us, please!' encored left flank.

Zara had quite turned her face away from them.

I thought I heard a whisper from her, an ancient incantation to keep secure what primeval man could keep faith with.

Air, Fire, Water, Stone.

Just keep it to the four elements we know well. We can live with those. And, we implore you, don't let the very ground give up its secrets.

'You'll be sure to see the Stones!' called the leader of the small pack, as she left us at the imposing entrance to the museum. It had been an early nineteenth century Primitive Methodist chapel in the local handsome dark stone.

I felt myself approving. They'd recycled it. Not religion any more, but a shrine nevertheless.

'Yes, isn't it?' said the young man who told me he was so glad to see us after he'd carefully inspected the letter the society had sent me. 'I'm Mr. Atkinson.'

'I have seen enough,' Zara said. 'I will wait outside.'

'Zara?'

'I need fresh air, Ben.'

The lighting showed the powerful features of the face, the thickness of the fingers, the frayed texture of the shreds of wolfskin cloak, and the way the thongs of the sandals had lapped their way up almost to the bones of the thick knees.

That bronze spear point in his back!

Had he howled his rage to the forested hills?

'Some guy?' asked Melissa. ''I wasn't expecting the size.'

Mr. Atkinson offered help.

'Two metres wasn't unusual then,' he said. 'If you got past infancy, you had a good chance of growing to a full height, and we know that lots of the men were much bigger than the present European average. Only the strong survived.'

'He didn't,' I found myself saying.

'Ah? I know that some of our more sensitive, or rather vulnerable, visitors can get a nasty turn just by one look at Our Harry — oh, shouldn't have said that! Sorry!'

Melissa and I were both curious.

We enquired about the name and we got an explanation. Someone on the committee had proposed it, and since calling the mummified corpse just The Bog Man seemed a bit callous, then Harry it was. It became *Ours*.

Our Harry.

Just the kind of bloke you'd come across down at the pub.

No. In a darker location altogether.

'Our Harry it is, then,' said Melissa. 'I see a Mr. Julius Fisk spent years on the dig. He isn't on the committee, I see?'

You'd have thought he'd have been on the committee, but he wasn't, according to the details we scanned in the pamphlet we bought from Atkinson.

Melissa asked about this.

'Well, it's difficult,' said the Curator. 'You see, it was private property, and at the time of Mr. Fisk's discovery, there was no right of public access. Yes, yes,' he said, forestalling our further questions.

He glibly explained that Julius Fisk was, after all, an *amateur*, whereas the Foundation took its responsibilities very seriously and completely *professionally*.

And no, they were out of postcards. The reprint could take a week or two.

'Poor old Fisk got zilch, then, Mr. Atkinson?'

'Leave it,' hissed Melissa.

I looked at my watch. An hour had passed.

'Zara!'

'I bought an ice-cream,' she said. 'The van comes for a few minutes every day about this time, then it goes. I talked to the boy who drives it. He's from Albania. He doesn't like England.'

'We go this way, Zara,' said Melissa.

She's the pathfinder.

'You sure you wouldn't prefer us all just to turn round and get on one of those slow trains back to Sheffield? Reggae and peppered chicken, maybe yams and hot chilli sauce, at Josh's?'

This was a newish, spare-looking place a mile out of the centre, with good food and good music, bring your own beer, wine if you preferred. Nothing hard, and no drugs, please. Josh was a short, burly, dreadlocked man who knew how to run a place. I think he'd looked Zara over with approval the last time we'd been there together.

'You're nice,' said Zara, leading the way up the winding track just past the church. 'We'll go on.'

I handed her my pack and got my shirt on. She gave me the pack back. There's a touch of the aristocrat about her.

Was.

'Onwards and upwards!'

'To the Stones,' said Melissa, doubtfully, I thought at the time.

'It's not a good time to be out in the dark,' came a voice seemingly from nowhere — a cracked, old man's voice, too.

We were alongside the graveyard.

Melissa screamed.

'Oh, my god!' Zara hung onto my arm.

Then we saw him.

He'd been in deep shadow. There was a huge old yew with thick densely leaved branches, and because we'd had the sun slanting in our eyes, he'd been invisible to us. He advanced on Zara.

'I said it's not a good time to be out in the dark for your kind.'

He was alone — an old, tall, thin creature, with legs like sticks and a green pack on his back and eyeglasses as thick as an old-fashioned beer bottle's base.

The Iranian girl who would have it that she was Persian wanted to talk to the spidery old man. It surprised me, for she had been badly shaken by the creaky warning from out of the gloom.

'Sir?'

'You should know,' he told her. 'Your kind do.'

I didn't like that, and he saw it.

'You think I have something against foreigners? Those of a different faith? Those who know the old ways?'

Melissa got between us.

'Sir? We apologise.'

'But they're just stones,' I said.

Well, *the* Stones.

Stones.

Twenty-one bits of rock.

'I say no more, but I think this young lady understands,' he told us, and I for one was glad to see the back of him.

'Ben. Let's move.'

'O.K.'

Ahead was a bleak landscape, made bleaker by the way the last of the sun's rays, which were golden-brown, with some crimson amongst low cloud, shone where the sheep had cropped what they could of the tufts of strong grasses.

The slanting sunlight enhanced its glow.

We made good time, and about forty minutes after the spidery-legged old man's warning, we got our first look into the cleft in the dark rock where the stones had been erected.

The Stones were weathered.

All except one.

' — eighteen, nineteen, twenty and one. And another!'

Melissa checked the pamphlet we'd bought at the museum.

'Someone's miscounted,' I said.

'Odd,' said Melissa.

'Twenty-two,' confirmed Zara.

'But it's not a Standing Stone. It's sort of leaning against the rocks. Doesn't count,' I said.

I checked again.

'This one's older rock,' I said. 'Here, Melissa. Look. And you, Zara.'

'No thanks,' I got from Zara.

I felt a rising of excitement. The leaning rock was a few metres from a cave.

'I wonder how far it goes into the rock. I'll have a look.'

'Don't, please, Ben. It isn't safe. Any shorings will have long since rotted away. You can get a roof fall at any time. It's an opening for the miners. Tin, maybe. Silver, probably. They all worked it, going back to the Phoenicians. They all used slave labour.'

'So why the extra stone?' I said. 'Twenty-one we should have, now one more. So, why?'

The sun was down, and I could see that Zara was shivering.

'What did that old guy mean, Zara? You know, down at the church.'

I had pondered the matter. He hadn't intentionally offended any of us. I knew that now.

Your kind?

The old ways?

I knew that her religion was incredibly ancient. The Persians had learned from their predecessors, the Avestans, and no one could quite put a date on their times. They had given the Persians the names of the twin and opposing forces, but at the time I couldn't recall the names Zara had told me about.

And, clearly, this wasn't the proper moment to question her.

'Please? May we leave it?'

I wanted to, but Melissa had become interested.

'Is it something to do with your beliefs, Zara?'

A heavy cloud was beginning to obscure the last of the red glow over the peaks. Zara hadn't answered Melissa. We were in a bad time. We all knew it.

And then, just like that, the mist came down, but it was a swirling, mote-filled mist, more of a — *miasma*. It was as though the air itself had been taken away from us.

Air.

'Ben?' said Melissa quietly.

Zara said something in her own

language, but I couldn't make out the syllables sufficiently well to give a form to the word. And when she repeated it, all I got was something like, 'A-ry-man!'

'It's getting darker,' muttered Melissa.

'A miasmic mist,' I said. 'That's all. We're in a deep little ravine, so it's bound to be darker down here.'

We all heard the howls at the same time. For my part, I had just hefted the packed rucksack onto my back, and I was still in an odd state in which I couldn't make up my mind as to whether we were under threat or not.

We were.

'What's that?' said Melissa. 'Dogs? Someone's dogs out there?'

The mist was colder; the light had almost gone.

'I suppose someone's walking their dogs, but it's late for that kind of thing. Maybe a couple of pets have got lost.'

'Not pets,' said Zara.

In the last of the dying light, I could see her face set in a stone-like gaze. I listened.

It wasn't a canine howl, no. Zara was right.

'We should move. Now!'

'Yes. Come on.'

But we had lost our sense of direction. The freezing mist had disoriented us.

'Ben!' cried Melissa.

I tripped and fell, my hands steadied by a rotting log that only served to make the impact against a stone outcrop all the worse. Consciousness left me as I cracked my head against the gritty stone. I heard Melissa's cry, probably after only two or three seconds of oblivion.

I saw torches in the darkness, and I glimpsed the faces of Furies.

'Ben!' screamed Melissa. 'It's those cursed bitches from the town!'

Bitches?

From the town?

They came out of the miasma, white and fat and naked: ten, a dozen, maybe more — bright red flares smoked and burned and revealed the bizarrely contorted faces of the women.

They were feral creatures.

I was hidden from their view, I realised.

The fallen log was part of a small barrier of rotted timbers, and the stone outcrop on which I had damaged my head gave additional cover. I was grateful for it.

'Ahriman!' I heard three or four yell, almost in unison.

'He will come!'

'We've got the Persian bitch!'

Persian, I said silently. *Not* Iranian. So they knew something at least of Zara's origins.

Then I knew: Zara had shrieked, in that strange Oriental way, the name of the evil being, the one implacably opposed to the forces of good.

Ahriman.

Melissa's despairing scream rocked me to the core of my being.

'Ben! Come to me!'

Triumphant calls came from the miasmic gloom.

'We've got the Fulham bitch, too. She's hiding in the pit!'

'Then roll the stone down on her. We'll keep her for later!'

The last was an instruction that was answered immediately by two or three of the hags. It was the leader again.

I reasoned some of it out in that

instant. Twenty-two stones, where there should be twenty-one.

A pit?

A stone lying by a pit?

I hadn't seen a pit, but we had found the entrance to one of the ancient diggings, hadn't we? Was that their *pit?*

That was as far as I got, for I risked a glance and saw that the snarling leader, torch held high to try to penetrate the awful gloom, was carrying in her right hand a gleaming hatchet.

My thoughts were clearing. I had some of it worked out.

Pit. Silver. A pre-Roman site. Bronze weapons.

A very old civilisation.

'He's here. Close by.'

I saw the flash of a sapphire ring.

Right flank.

A vivid red: a coral necklace.

Left flank.

'He won't get far,' the leader said, regaining some measure of control. 'Ahriman comes!'

It was long past time for me to do my part. I felt the flow of blood through my arms and legs. My strength was returning. I got to my feet and drove myself forward. A break in the mist showed me a terrible sight.

The Stones were the background to an evil that should not exist in the Dark Peak, but which was there before my staring eyes. Zara was naked.

She was quite alone, ringed by a pack of Harpies, all brandishing torches and all too carried away by their blood-lust to note my emergence from my hiding-place.

The cry was loudest from the leader of the hags.

' — riman, come!'

The hag-bitch thrust her left hand out, almost into Zara's long, black hair.

Then Zara moved.

She reached for the flare.

She called on the force of light, the Zoroastrian twin and opposing deity.

'Ozmud!'

'Ahriman!' shrieked the bitch-hag.

She reached to her burned eyes, dropping the hatchet and yelling in appalled rage at the Persian woman who had blinded her.

I felt the blow halfway up my back.

I knew what it was. The spear point was in my spine. A violent event from three millennia ago was being repeated. I was down again, my head crashing against something hard. I fell into water.

I had been concussed before, hurt badly. But not like this.

What could I do?

I tumbled, fell and sank into water and oblivion.

Josh could forget his hopes of Zara, for I heard the terrible noises that spoke of the manner of her death.

She got —

There is a word that is not often used, but pathologists know it: they have to deal with the aftermath. It is *rended*.

Then I felt the weight of the rucksack. It wasn't much of a burden. I thought to throw it off before I went in pursuit of my own form of vengeance.

The spear lay beside me, the point embedded in both the cell-phone and the strong metal casing of the first aid box. Those, and the thickness of heavy-duty, old-fashioned canvas had saved me.

'Move,' I grunted, and leapt towards the hellish circle and the *thing* that was throwing body parts to them.

'Ahriman!' they screamed.

Our Harry.

Of course.

That was their utterly sick and contemptuous way of giving the awakened devil a harmless, old-fashioned name. The kind of bloke you met —

'Zara!' I roared.

I hefted the spear. I can throw things hard: javelins, shot, and cricket balls, whatever is needed.

It should have hit him square in the throat, but this thing at one time had been a warrior.

Slave master or mine owner?

Escapee or pursuer, himself to be pursued and hunted to a cold death in a deep bog that would turn to peat and mummify him — *it!*

He eased aside, and the spear thudded into the tufted grass a foot from his right. Then he was up and drawing a long, heavy knife from a skin scabbard: a hunter in the lead, and a pack of hell hags screeching in his wake. They left the fighting to their grim champion.

I ran at him, arms outstretched to rip his glaring eyes from his bearded, shaggy head, and his head from his shoulders, then tear him apart and send him back into the mists of time. I think he could have killed me within two seconds. But I would have marked him, torn some part of his long-dead corpse away — an arm, maybe a leg, if I could tangle with him.

We were near to clashing, when a hand feebly grasped my ankle and momentarily checked me. I swung aside from the beast's charge and the blinded leader of the hags swung at me with a glittering edged weapon in her free hand. She sobbed her loyalty to it.

I put my shoulder down and caught it in a fierce grinding of bone and muscle.

Then we were on the ground, rolling in the bracken and grass, the thing stabbing and yelling — its breath reeking of the charnel house; its long, bloodied incisors searching to tear out my jugular vein. I am strong, but this *thing* had iron tendons and stone bones. Its weight was more than mine, and its ferocity out-matched anything that even the fear of death could bring me to.

I reached out a hand to ward off the flint knife.

I rolled away in a free moment.

The hags screamed in triumph.

The leader yelled in pain.

My hand felt a long, smooth handle.

Hatchet.

Edged weapon.

Hers.

I swung, harder than I have ever swung at anything.

The blade sank deep into the iron tendons, cutting through gore-matted beard and hair, slicing easily into the thick veins of the neck, and only half-stopping at the intersection of skull and vertebrae.

The Bog Man's mouth opened. I saw the fangs.

It tried to roar. Then it dropped the flint knife and instinctively raised both hands to the throat.

'Die again!'

I swung, just as hard, and the thing's

head rocked on the torso and then fell away into the smoke and mist. The twice-dead headless corpse remained upright for a moment, and then it slowly toppled away, to fall at the feet of the hag who had tried to slice my belly open. I held still in shock.

She must have had some partial sight, for she reached out to the thing and placed her head at the pumping junction where head and body should have been.

What was she doing?

I reeled. I was almost exhausted. I was back in my place, one with the rest of humanity. But the hag bitch's cautious movements held me in a spell. Simply, I couldn't do the things that needed my attention.

What was she doing now?

She reached into the grass in what seemed to be almost tender carefulness, then her hands discovered the thing's head. She reached for it, held it in her two large hands and then crushed it to her bloodied breasts in a wild protective movement, as if she could comfort the *thing* and restore it to some form of life.

She keened over the head for a second or two.

Then I recovered my wits. I could do nothing for poor, infinitely courageous Zara, but I could rescue my woman.

'Kill!' screamed back the hag pack.

'Stones!' shrieked the burned woman. 'Stone him!'

I half-raised the edged weapon. I could kill some of them, wound more. But there was a pack of them, and they held pieces of grit stone in their hands. I heard a call as they armed themselves.

Melissa!

'Melissa!' I called back, but my voice was without power.

'In the cave!'

The first flight of stones was badly aimed. One glanced off my left shoulder. It hurt and helped at the same time. These were not ordinary upper-class Englishwomen. They were ghouls.

But could I leave Melissa under the Stone?

No.

Never.

It was, then, a fight to the death.

Against a shower of heavy stones, I must soon be knocked down. How many could I kill by a berserker charge?

Not enough.

And then came a colossal blast of sound that had us all confounded. It was the unmistakable roar of a modern, heavy weapon. It filled the valley and left a ringing silence. And it had stopped the women in their tracks. Rocks fell from their nerveless hands. Like me, they knew the sound of a shotgun's blast.

'This is a repeating shotgun,' called a reedy, old man's voice. 'I have six rounds left, and a belt of ammunition on my shoulder!'

'Fisk!' hissed the half-blinded woman.

'You will all go now!'

'Never!' she shrieked back.

For answer, he blasted the headless torso lying beside her.

'You die, Fisk!' she screamed.

'Leave the head!'

Another blast of sound filled the ravine.

The head rolled away. I saw its fangs for the last time.

Fisk knew what to do, and in a matter

of three or four minutes we had prised the twenty-second out. Melissa choked, spat dust out and told me that she was never again going to let me out of her sight, if she could help it.

The rest of it was difficult.

'Zara? No!'

She didn't want to believe it. She was traumatised. But we helped one another down into the town and then collapsed. Fisk turned to us:

'Forget tonight. All of it. For your very souls' sake! Say nothing! They will know!'

I got delayed concussion. That's how the paramedics found me. I was unconscious for the next thirty-six hours. I asked for Melissa and Zara. One traumatised and with her parents in Fulham. Regretfully, one mauled to death. Then, a calm Divisional Superintendent of police came to take my statement at the hospital.

'Really sir, a dozen naked women? Shotguns and spears? A savage, you say, sir? I'll let you recover. I'll come back. You rest, sir.'

I was a hero and the medical staff

regarded me with some awe. In the press, none of it had happened as we had experienced it.

The detective came back after I had been sedated for half a day.

'Fisk? He was there! Without him, we'd all be dead!'

'We're all truly sorry about Mr. Julius Fisk, sir. He had a heart attack only yesterday. Fatal, I'm afraid. You ready to make a — well, a proper statement now you've rested, sir?'

For your very souls' sake!

'Accusations of murder?' he said. 'That, sir, is the most serious matter of all. But our Scene of Crime Officers have already been over the ground most carefully. And I can assure you that what has emerged has been exactly what was first reported in the newspapers. We found evidence of a terrible assault and mutilation, yes, but it was clear that the marauding large cat killed the young lady. We found it headless, and the creature's head nearby. Ferocious beast! It's been marauding in these parts for over a year. Took very many sheep, and threatened the lives of more than one child. You're a brave young man.'

'Puma? It was the damned Bog Man!'

'Sir, let's be reasonable. We are all most grateful to you.'

They gave me sedatives again and I blacked out for two more days.

Melissa came to see me.

'Sorry,' she said. 'I had a sort of breakdown. My dad came for me.'

'But you're back.'

'Forever, Ben. Don't talk about it now. Let's go home.'

'What do we do?' I said. 'Newspapers? Television? Channel Five?'

For your very souls' sake!

But Zara needed to be avenged!

I asked Melissa to corroborate my story.

'They won't believe us, Ben.'

'Someone has to!'

We set out our story for the media. *Sorry*.

Our story of wild naked middle-aged women was not even considered seriously by them. Were we looking for a payout? That was their view: that we had further sensationalised a truly ghastly killing, dressing it up with rumours and legends and a bit of archaeological evidence. The police had given them all the facts they wanted, and no thanks.

And there would be no payouts, of course.

I gave it three days and went back to Grysethorpe.

Melissa said she couldn't take any more. Three distant cousins of Zara's had turned up from Paris and angrily told me they didn't want any more stories about her. They would see that she was cared for properly when her body was released after the inquest. They treated us with some suspicion and left.

For your very souls' sake!

No. I had to go on.

It was raining when I got off the train at the tidy station. The wind hit me in the face as I walked along the only street and turned the corner as we three had on that fateful day.

I was unsurprised to see that the place was boarded up. A neat notice informed visitors that the place was closed so that repairs could be carried out. I banged on the door and called for Fisk. There was no answer. I looked through the windows at street level, but they had been fitted with drapes where they were not covered in heavy-duty boarding. I looked up to a small window just below the stone arch of the old chapel.

And I saw her.

It was the leader of the hags.

It was just a glimpse, but I have keen eyes and I know that in that single instant she recognised me. The face was badly scarred, and there was just one glittering eye to glare at me. I backed away, appalled.

'A burned lady with one eye, sir?' asked Gryesthorpe's only policeman at the police house. 'That must be Lady Seymour-Fitzgerald, sir. Very good family. Friends of the Lord Lieutenant. Distressing accident. Bad thing, that.'

'I saw them. Her.'

He believed me! But he was local, so he would know of the damned hell-hags. 'I never recommend these gas cylinder barbecue kits. Blow up. And blow up it did, the poor lady.'

It was a cover-up. It had been from the start.

They'd found a puma, and cut its head off.

'Like to have a photograph of the head, sir? You have a good eye with an axe, I'll say that. But I gather you're a cricketer? Two nice cuts to mid off, those!'

'How about the axe?'

He told me.

'Boy Scout camp near here, you see, and someone got careless and they lost a hatchet cutting woodfalls near the Stones. We'll keep it as evidence for a while. Anything else, sir?'

'About Mr. Julius Fisk.'

'Thought the Super had told you, sir. Heart attack, it was. You all right, sir?'

'I see the museum's undergoing repairs.'

'Vandals, that. We don't get many here. I see to that! But Mr. Atkinson couldn't take it and left.'

He was in the cover-up. I could do no more.

I got Fisk's letter the next day. It arrived by hand courtesy of his housekeeper. She said she should really have given it to the police, but it had been his wish that I be found and receive it. At the hospital they'd been sympathetic and since I was such a hero they'd bend the rules a bit and forward Fisk's letter to me. It wasn't long. I won't give anything but the gist of it.

It was a cult thing.

In pointless lives ancient desires had stirred in their heavy bosoms and ponderous bellies. Primeval thrills had suffused them. But don't underestimate their powers. And don't be too surprised if I'm not around for much longer.

They'd sniffed out Zara and her beliefs. Her beliefs were diametrically opposed to the strange creature they could revive at intervals. Probably, said Fisk, he had been a shaman from the area known as Mesopotamia: they thought of the god as a diabolical creature who could come back and take over the remains of one of his followers. The hags had not been able to resist this summons.

And, always, they needed blood.

Fisk's letter ended succinctly: 'Go. Now. As far as you can.'

The postcard was unsigned:

'We look forward to seeing you two.'

I knew that when I got the postcard and saw the frightful picture.

It was the Bog Man. He was in his crypt at the museum. The head was totally detached from the torso.

Melissa shrieked.

The post also had the hoped-for letter from Marine Gendives, based at Cairns. Would I undertake some work on a two-year contract that involved diving on the Reef, and could I come soon? Liked your work on the mollusc genome. Come on, mate.

'Get a visa from Australia House,' I told Melissa. 'You've still got student status. We can be on a plane in two days.'

The phone rang. We looked at one another.

'I'll take it,' I said.

'How nice you're still with us,' came that familiar cut-glass voice, that of the leader of the hags.

Melissa caught the tones.

'Pack,' I told her. 'Five minutes and we're out.'

'Zara?'

'We'll always remember her.'

'Us?'

'Together.'

'Them?'

'It's a new world. We'll leave this one behind.'

The phone rang again. We left it.

For your very souls' sake.

Ours.

THE END